By Lisa Yee

Random House New York

To my Mom and Dad. Thank you
for always encouraging me to dream.

# PROLOGUE

"**W**ONDER WOMAN!" Principal Waller bellowed.

Wonder Woman blinked several times, unable to comprehend what was happening. The cheering ramped up, along with a snide remark—or two—from Cheetah,who yawned and stretched with the grace of a ballerina, accidentally-on-purpose bumping Katana, who immediately shoved her back. Luckily, the auditorium, along with all the other buildings at Super Hero High, was built to withstand invaders, firestorms, comets, and teenagers.

"Wonder Woman, please join me on the stage," the principal said again, suppressing a smile. It did not behoove her to appear too cheerful. After all, Amanda "The Wall" Waller prided herself on running Super Hero High with so much strength and conviction that there was no room for frivolity. With her massive shoulders, severe suits, and no-nonsense haircut, Waller's mere presence was enough to shut down an entire fleet of alien interlopers—or a room packed with rambunctious super-heroes-in-training.

Harley Quinn of the "Harley's Quinntessentials" channel on ViewTube laughed and began recording as Bumblebee buzzed over to Wonder Woman and guided her toward the stage. "Go, Wondy!" Bumblebee shouted gleefully as her yellow wings lifted her off the ground. "You know Waller hates to be kept waiting!"

The normally gregarious Wonder Woman stood stunned as she listened to Principal Waller. The gold tiara nestled into her long, thick black hair glistened.

"This 'Hero of the Month' has brought pride and dedication to our school," The Wall continued. "She is not here for personal glory, but for the greater good, and to shine the spotlight on others. *That* is what a true leader does."

By now Wonder Woman was choking back tears. She had only been at Super Hero High for a few months. Her mother, Hippolyta, Queen of Themyscira, aka Paradise Island, would be so proud. She couldn't wait to talk to her. "Wonder Woman," she could hear Waller saying, "for your first assignment as Hero of the Month, you will be showing our newest Super Hero High student around the school. Oh! Here she comes now!"

There was a gasp from the crowd. Wonder Woman smiled. Cheetah frowned. Harley Quinn videoed.

The rumors were true!

# PART ONE

# CHAPTER 1

It seemed like forever since she'd been hurtling through space for whereabouts unknown. Her spacecraft hadn't taken the fastest, most direct route, but it eventually got her where she needed to be. She had little memory of the journey. Instead, her thoughts kept going back to when she had been happy and carefree, to the point of taking so much of her life for granted. . . .

Several solar systems away from Earth and to the left, a young girl had almost been finished making a birthday card for her mom when emergency alarms sounded. Kara had heard these practice drills all her life and paid little attention to them. But when her mother burst into her room, the panic in her eyes told Kara that today was different.

"Kara!" her mom cried, out of breath. "Hurry! Come with me, now!"

Without asking questions, Kara grabbed her mother's hand and ran, dropping the card behind her. She had written

"To the best mom in the universe" but hadn't had time to add "Love always, Kara."

Her father was pacing outside by the spaceship. For a brief second, his face softened with relief when he saw his daughter; then it grew serious again. "Kara, get in," he ordered. His normally soft, comforting voice was replaced with one she had never heard before. It scared her. "There's no time! GET IN NOW!"

As the crushing sound of emergency alarms rang ever louder, Kara Zor-El of the planet Krypton did as she was told. She felt her heart racing as the spaceship began to shudder—but it hadn't taken off. It was the vibration of her entire planet quaking from its very core. Her mother's hands trembled as she placed a crystal necklace around Kara's neck. "We love you, Kara. More than you can ever imagine," she said.

Kara's father joined them for an embrace.

"But, Mom, I don't understand!" Kara said in a panic. In the entryway to the spacecraft, her parents hugged her even tighter. "What's happening? Did I do something wrong?"

"You have done nothing wrong," her mother said, gently brushing the blond bangs from her daughter's eyes. Worry was etched on her face. "Always do your best, Kara, and you'll be fine. I promise. You have the heart of a hero."

Her parents were always so wise and strong. Nothing could have prepared Kara for their tears as they strapped her into the ship's lone command chair and stepped away. Suddenly, the door was sealed shut with Kara inside . . . alone. She pressed her hands against the glass and her mother did the same on the other side. Her father pulled her mom away only seconds before the spaceship blasted off.

Before Kara could take in what was happening, there was an explosion so loud and powerful that it jolted the spacecraft, already barreling into the darkness. Debris pounded the tiny vessel, causing it to spin like the hands of a crazed cuckoo clock. If Kara had not been wearing a seat belt, she surely would have been tossed like a rag doll within the close confines of the ship. Instead, she was merely knocked unconscious.

Little did Kara know that her ship had veered massively off course at a velocity surpassing the speed of light. And at that speed, time did some pretty strange things, as Kara would find out.

When Kara finally woke, the silence consumed her. She would rather have heard the deafening sounds of the debris hitting the spacecraft—at least that would have taken her mind off what was happening. From the control panel, Kara could tell she was headed for Earth, a planet 21.7 light-years away and populated by a species of aliens known as humans.

On autopilot, the spaceship finally began to slow as it neared the Earth's atmosphere. From her window, Kara watched the blue marble of a planet draw closer. When the yellow sun hit the horizon, a crest of glowing gold arched over its surface. As she got closer, Kara could see vast fields of blue, swirls of white, and patches of green. Mountains and oceans soon appeared. Incredibly, if she focused, Kara could zoom in on wild mustangs galloping across plains, traffic clogging cities, and houses with happy families inside. Her gaze lingered on these the longest.

But just then, the emergency warning signal began to blare and the spacecraft started shaking uncontrollably as it entered the Earth's atmosphere. Kara hoped for the best as she braced herself for the worst.

# CHAPTER 2

**D**eep in America's heartland, where golden stalks of wheat reached toward the big blue sky, teenager Kara Zor-El felt alone. Though the tidy yellow house was endlessly cheery, she could only pretend to be.

Kara wiped away her tears with the back of her hand as she glanced at the freshly painted purple bedroom full of stuffed animals, some with their price tags still on, and posters of the most popular bands. Even though she'd been told that this was her room, Kara longed to go home. But that was impossible.

Smallville, Kansas, USA, Earth, was a long way from Krypton, just as another orphaned Kryptonian had learned a long time ago. . . .

When their planet exploded, he had been sent to Earth as an infant but had grown to become his adopted planet's greatest hero. The Kents were the Earth people who had taken him in, raised him, and loved him as their own. And when his superpowered senses had detected Kara's craft crashing into the atmosphere, he had rescued her and brought her to live with his family.

But how was he almost a grown man while she was still a teenager, when they had both left Krypton at the same time? "Differing trajectories through space . . . wormholes and the like," he offered as possibilities to explain it to a still perplexed Kara. The route she had traveled from their doomed planet had taken a lot longer than Superman's, and she'd arrived on Earth almost twenty years after her fellow Kryptonian!

"There is so much I can tell you when the time is right," Superman said as he'd set her down on the couch in the Kents' living room. Aunt Martha and Uncle Jonathan looked on anxiously. "But for now you need to adjust to life here on Earth. You'll have powers you aren't aware of yet, and they will grow under the Earth's yellow sun. Use them wisely, Kara. You are safe and in good hands here. I promise."

Before she could speak, Superman was gone.

★

So much of Kara's life had been turned upside down and inside out. Her planet and all she had known and loved had been destroyed. The one comfort she had was the crystal necklace her mother had given her.

As kind as Aunt Martha and Uncle Jonathan were, Kara could tell they felt sorry for her. And the truth was, she felt sorry for herself. Who could blame her? Imagine, one moment you're making a card for your mom, and the next you're being blasted off into space—and through the small round window in your spaceship, you are the sole witness to your planet's destruction.

Knowing that the Kents were trying to show her every possible kindness, Kara tried hard to appear happy and optimistic. Without them having to ask, she helped out around the house and on the farm. Here was a girl who didn't even like making her bed on Krypton, now volunteering to do the laundry! But things were different here. It wasn't like home.

Something strange had happened to Kara in the short time since she'd landed on Earth. As Superman had warned her, she was now in possession of superpowers so intense she was afraid to sneeze, for fear she'd destroy something, or someone. Kara didn't even know how many powers she had. They were growing at a rate faster than she or the Kents could have imagined. The first time she picked up some eggs from the henhouse, they cracked at her touch. When the Kents needed help herding a trio of stray cows, Kara accidentally tossed one into the sky. Luckily, she caught the startled cow before it hit the ground. And then there was the first time she tried out her heat vision. The beams from Kara's eyes were so powerful that when they hit the cornfield, popcorn rained over the tiny town of Smallville, much to the delight of the drive-in movie patrons.

Yet, despite the accidents, there was one superpower Kara couldn't get enough of: *flying.* Careful at first to stay near the Kent farm, she flew only a few states away. Later, she would fly higher and farther, testing herself. When in flight, she was at peace, able to remember her mother and father and the home the three of them had shared. Now, home was with Aunt Martha and Uncle Jonathan, she had to remind herself. But as caring and accepting as they were, the Kents' kindness made Kara miss her parents even more.

The short time Kara Zor-El spent on the Kent farm was like being in a cocoon—warm and safe, albeit with her powers growing rapidly out of control. At night, before bed, she often thought about how a whole lifetime ago, her life had changed. And though Kara didn't know it, it was about to change again.

# CHAPTER 3

As the weeks went on, Kara fell into a routine. Rising early to help on the farm, eating delicious home-cooked meals, going to bed tired after a full day of stacking bales of hay, lifting farm machines, and building miles of fences. "It's just like if Clark were here," Aunt Martha said, calling Kara's fellow Kryptonian Superman by his Earth name.

"He's a good boy," Uncle Jonathan said as he polished one of Superman's trophies. "And he's doing well in college, even though they've got him busy all the time."

"Speaking of school," Aunt Martha said carefully, "Kara, it's time you started getting ready for high school. We've enjoyed every minute of having you here, but . . ."

Uncle Jonathan nodded, but his eyes looked concerned as Aunt Martha continued. "Well, we were thinking of Super Hero High. You should be with kids your own age. Plus, as much as we love you, there's only so much we can do to help you control your powers. You need to be with experts who can guide you. We're just mere mortals."

Kara looked up from the sketchpad where she was doodling a picture of her parents. The Kents were more than mere mortals, she thought. They were Aunt Martha and Uncle Jonathan, and she felt safe with them. Were they trying to get rid of her? Kara knew that her attempts at helping out often caused mayhem. Was this about that incident with the grain silo? She hadn't meant for it to tip over when she accidentally flew into it. When a video of her setting it back on its foundation had been posted online, some people started saying that the girl in the video was Superman's cousin, and had even taken to calling her Supergirl.

"But Superman got to stay here for years," Kara began to protest.

"Dear girl," Aunt Martha said. "Your cousin came to us as a baby, and as he grew, so did his superpowers. They developed slowly over several years."

"But you, Kara," Uncle Jonathan said, piping in, "your powers are more than any of us could have imagined. And they keep getting stronger each day."

Kara had known that she was going to have to go to school eventually. Her parents would have wanted that. But she had thought that maybe Korugar Academy, located several sectors away, would be a good choice for her. Some of the galaxy's most powerful teens went there. And like her, most of them were aliens in one way or another. Maybe there she wouldn't feel so . . . out of place. Yet the Kents seemed set on her going to Superman's alma mater. "Just look at the website," Uncle Jonathan encouraged her.

"I think you'll like it," Aunt Martha added, smiling warmly at Kara.

Kara tried to return the smile.

Back in her room, Kara leaned forward as she watched the Super Hero High recruitment video. To her surprise, despite her initial hesitation, she found herself drawn to the school. It looked inviting and exciting, and everyone seemed friendly. She couldn't help getting swept away in the enthusiasm as she clicked through several pages on the school website. The ones Kara liked most featured Wonder Woman. The Amazon warrior princess was so strong and confident. So self-assured. Unlike Kara, Wonder Woman looked like she had everything under control. Kara also read articles about Wonder Woman by a teen reporter named Lois Lane on the *Daily Planet*'s website that covered some of the hero's epic saves when danger threatened the city of Metropolis.

Eager to find out more, Kara clicked on a link to something called "Harley's Quinntessentials," featuring a pigtailed girl named Harley Quinn who promised "All Harley, all the time, giving you the latest in Teen Super Hero News, Notes, and Gossip!" She watched one video, then another and another and another. There seemed to be an endless supply of "Harley's Quinntessentials" segments of Super Hero High students crashing into walls and one another, overturning armored cars by accident, causing havoc in the chemistry lab, and having bad hair days. Kara loved the laughs the clips gave her—especially because they made her feel like she wasn't the clumsiest kid on the planet.

But still, she thought wistfully, if she could just be a little more like Wonder Woman, then maybe she'd fit in. Even on the "Harley's Quinntessentials" blooper reels, Wonder Woman looked regal.

Kara adjusted the headband that kept her hair out of her face and tied the laces on her red high-top sneakers. She looked at herself in the mirror and straightened her blue shirt with her family crest in the center. Clearing her throat, she extended her hand and practiced saying, "Nice to meet you, Wonder Woman. My name is Kara Zor-El." Then, on a whim, she tried out, "My name is . . . Supergirl."

Maybe going to Super Hero High was a good idea after all.

★

Kara spent the rest of the afternoon researching. Super Hero High had just won the 100th Super Triathlon, thanks to Wonder Woman and her team, and it was known for its reputation of training the best and brightest young super heroes. Just look at how well her cousin had done for himself.

On the other hand, Korugar Academy boasted an extensive roster of powerful and famous alumni, too. *And* there were no tests.

But Super Hero High had Wonder Woman. Plus, its principal, Amanda Waller, had reached out to Kara personally, sending her a video invitation that said "I sincerely hope you'll join our Super Hero High family."

Then again, Korugar Academy was known for having lots of transfer students. It had one of the highest enrollments of aliens in the solar system.

It was a difficult decision. But it was one she would have to make for herself. Whatever school Kara picked would surely have a big impact on her life.

"Kara! It's time to go. Are you ready?" Aunt Martha called from the bottom of the stairs, bringing her back to reality.

"Yes, be right there," Kara yelled back.

Using her X-ray vision, she scanned her room for her suitcase and saw it buried under a pile of blankets and clothes. Like a whirlwind, Kara packed and cleaned the room, and mere moments later, she was at the top of the stairwell.

"Here I come," she called out, right before tripping and tumbling down the stairs. Her suitcase went flying, opening in midair and sending everything spilling out, including a brochure for Korugar Academy.

"Thank you for considering Korugar Academy!" a robotic voice intoned from the brochure as it sailed through the room. "Located in space sector 1417, Korugar is your far-off destination for higher education! We are a test-optional school! No grades! You will become your best because we accept nothing less. Join us at Korugar Academy!"

As Kara tried to catch her falling suitcase and its contents, she bounced against the walls, breaking furniture, destroying Aunt Martha's collection of ceramic owls, and bowling down Uncle Jonathan's shelves of antique railroad lanterns.

"Well, that was impressive!" Aunt Martha said as she crawled out from under the dining room table.

Kara surveyed the destruction. It looked as though a hurricane had blown through the house. Maybe it had—and its name was Supergirl.

"Thank you for helping us dispose of these old things," Aunt Martha said cheerfully. "This gives us an excuse to redecorate!"

Uncle Jonathan came in from the barn and surveyed the room. "Nice job!" he said, unfazed by the mess.

Supergirl hung her head, embarrassed.

"Super Hero High will help you control your powers," Aunt Martha promised, putting an arm around her. "You're going to love it there."

"They graduate the best super heroes in the business," Uncle Jonathan added confidently.

Doubt washed over Kara. She knew that Super Hero High had sky-high standards. The rigorous training, the endless tests, the pressure to succeed . . . She was just a girl from Krypton who couldn't control her most basic abilities. What if she didn't want to be a super hero? Had anyone asked her about that?

*How can I be a super hero?* Kara wondered. *I can't even save my super self from being such a super mess.*

She looked at the Korugar Academy brochure on the floor. It was saying "Join us . . . join us . . . join us . . ." Kara snatched it up and threw it away, hoping the Kents hadn't seen it.

Kara bid her aunt and uncle goodbye and began her ascent into the sky, suitcase in hand. She flew around the planet a couple of times to help shake off her uncertainty. As she looked down, Kara noted how beautiful the Earth was. It was like a colorful quilt stitched together with many remarkable cultures and landscapes. Using her super-hearing, she tuned in on the music across the continents, pausing to listen to a girl about her age playing the violin with such passion that it made Kara stronger just listening to it.

Instinctively, Kara clutched her crystal necklace. The necklace began to glow. If only her parents could experience this. Her father had always wanted to travel. She wished they could experience this together.

"You have the heart of a hero," she could hear her mother saying. "Always do your best, Kara, and you'll be fine. I promise."

With her mother's words ringing in her ears, Kara flew faster. As she crossed each country, she felt braver, more confident, and eager to start anew. Soon, she pierced the clouds, waving as she shot past airplanes, and soared toward a city called Metropolis, where a new life awaited her.

# CHAPTER 4

One hundred miles out, using her telescopic vision, Kara spotted the warm, welcoming glow of the high school's iconic Amethyst Tower. Holding on to her suitcase with one hand, she instinctively gripped her crystal necklace with the other. It lit up as bright as the Amethyst. Before landing, Kara paused to peer down through an opening in the clouds. She recognized Harley Quinn from "Harley's Quinntessentials," doing cartwheels toward the main building. The sight of Harley gave her a giddy feeling, and suddenly she couldn't wait to be a part of Super Hero High. Energized, Kara dived down, shouting, "Yoo-hoo! Hellooooo!" She lifted a hand to wave . . . and dropped her suitcase in the process.

Kara swooped in the air to catch it but only succeeded in crashing into Amethyst Tower, bouncing off the cafeteria, and landing in a heap on the ground, with her belongings scattered all over the school.

"Are you okay?"

Everything was spinning. Kara sat up and opened her eyes. She was certain she was seeing things—or *not* seeing them! She could hear a voice, but where was it coming from? Then she saw it: a tiny bee buzzing around her. Kara waved her arms to swat it away.

"Hey!" the bee yelled.

Kara stared as the bee grew into a girl about the same size as her. The super hero's yellow wings glistened in the sunlight, and her black hair was streaked with golden tresses the color of honey.

"I'm Bumblebee. I'm not going to hurt you," the girl said. Her voice was friendly and her smile genuine. She motioned to a girl with flowing red hair wearing a green frock over green leggings. "That's Poison Ivy. We're here to help!"

Poison Ivy knelt down and handed a bunch of flowers to Kara, motioning for her to sniff. "The scent from these flowers can help heal you," she said, barely meeting Kara's gaze.

Kara buried her nose in the bouquet and took a deep breath, relishing the floral perfume. She felt better already.

"Thanks. I'm . . . I'm Supergirl."

There.

She'd actually said it.

She had called herself Supergirl!

But before Supergirl could embrace the moment, a large shadow fell over her.

Poison Ivy and Bumblebee jumped to attention.

"Students, initiate damage control protocol!" a woman's voice bellowed. Supergirl recognized Principal Amanda Waller from the school's videos. "Wonder Woman, you're on Amethyst inspection!"

Supergirl gasped. Heading straight toward the tower was none other than Wonder Woman! In person! She flew with the confidence and determination that Supergirl could only dream of possessing one day. She desperately wanted to meet her—but Wonder Woman was too focused on her task to stop and chat.

"Bumblebee, check for microscopic damage," Waller continued. "Barbara! Where is Barbara Gordon?"

"Here!" an auburn-haired girl called out. She adjusted her glasses, then pulled a microcomputer from her Utility Belt. "I know, check the electrical. I'm already on it!"

The principal turned to a large gorilla lumbering toward them. His sport jacket was slightly too small. The buttons threatened to pop any moment. A red handkerchief was tucked into his breast pocket. "Vice Principal Grodd, you got this?" she asked. The gorilla grunted and nodded as he munched on a bamboo stalk.

"Double-check everything," Waller ordered. "Any crack could be disastrous. This Amethyst contains more energy than a nuclear power plant—enough energy to amplify a villain's arsenal a hundredfold. The assembly's starting soon. I have to go! Someone assist the new girl!"

Still clutching the flowers, Supergirl sat up with the help of Poison Ivy and Bumblebee. Putting on a bright smile, she assured them, "I'm fine. Really, I am!"

"I'm not so sure about that," Poison Ivy said. "We'll walk with you to the auditorium. There's going to be a big announcement!"

# CHAPTER 5

As she was ushered into the auditorium, Supergirl looked around at the other teens. Everyone seemed comfortable with one another, whether they were humans, aliens, machines, animals, or a combination. Supergirl used to have a lot of friends on Krypton. She was known for her friendliness and optimism. In another world and time, this could have been her high school. Instead, she was the new girl.

Determined to make a good impression, Supergirl took a deep breath and turned her sadness into a smile. There was a hushed silence when Waller began talking about the school's Hero of the Month. Everyone was facing forward, on the edge of their seats.

"WONDER WOMAN!" the principal called out. Supergirl gripped the wall as crashing cheers rocked the auditorium.

Onstage, Wonder Woman, with a combination of power and grace, accepted the Hero of the Month award. She was even more charismatic in person than in the videos.

"Wonder Woman, as one of your first duties as Hero of the Month, you will show our newest student around Super Hero High," Waller informed her.

New student?

Supergirl stood up straight. Before the principal even finished her sentence, she was bounding up the aisle with such enthusiasm that she tripped over her shoelaces and tumbled out of control. She knocked over several teachers, who then crashed into Commissioner Gordon and another teacher, who slammed into the first two rows of students and sent them flying wildly into the air. Chaos erupted as Harley Quinn let out a raucous laugh and caught it all on camera for "Harley's Quinntessentials."

The airborne Supers recovered before they hit the ground, and in spectacular fashion righted themselves and maneuvered to save their classmates. The school's other flyers also swooped in to assist midair, turning the disaster into an impressive synchronized save.

Supergirl ran over to Wonder Woman, stumbling twice, but jumping up each time as if nothing had happened. Her eyes bright, she held out her hand.

"I am a huge, huge, huge fan!" Supergirl gushed. "I am *sooooo* excited to meet you, Wonder Woman. I hope we can be friends! Can we? Please say yes!"

"Yes, of course," Wonder Woman said, smiling.

Supergirl's blue eyes sparkled with happiness.

As the students cheered, Principal Waller straightened

25

the collar of her slate-gray suit and cleared her throat to silence them. "Supergirl," she said, regaining control of the room. "Welcome to Super Hero High. We hope you'll enjoy your new school and excel in your studies. Wonder Woman will be here to assist you with anything you need." Wonder Woman smiled at Supergirl, who smiled back. "Is there anything you'd like to say to your fellow students? Anything you'd like them to know about you?"

Supergirl looked out over the audience. All eyes were on her. Should she tell them that she lost her parents and her planet? Or that she was nervous about being the new student at such a prestigious high school? And that she was scared?

Everyone was waiting for her to speak. Supergirl looked at Wonder Woman, who nodded at her encouragingly. She gulped and then said brightly, "I am so thrilled to be here at Super Hero High. And sooooo, sooooo sorry that I tripped. In fact, if you'd rather call me Super Klutz instead of Supergirl, I'd totally understand!"

Warm laughter swept the room, and Supergirl soaked in the smiles.

That afternoon, true to her word, Wonder Woman took Supergirl around, showing her the school, introducing her to the students and staff, and even giving her valuable insight into confusing things.

"This is cereal," Wonder Woman said as they walked through the dining hall. Supergirl admired the brightly colored shapes and sizes housed in clear, thick, tall tubes. "We can eat all we want! I like to mix the flavors."

Supergirl nodded. She wondered if she ate a lot of cereal, would she be more like Wonder Woman?

"Those are boys," Wonder Woman said, pointing to Green Lantern and The Flash.

"Hey, Wonder Woman," The Flash called out, giving her a friendly wave. "Welcome to Super Hero High," he said to Supergirl.

Wonder Woman whispered to Supergirl. "Boys are exactly the same as us girls, only different."

Supergirl nodded. She had heard that before.

"That's the library," Wonder Woman continued. "Almost every book in the world you could want is in there."

*Every book?* Supergirl mused. "Even books about Krypton?"

"What was that?" Wonder Woman asked, leaning in.

Supergirl was suddenly hit with a bout of shyness. After all, here was her idol taking her around school, and even talking to her as if they were friends. *I could really use a friend,* Supergirl thought.

"When you meet someone new, you shake hands with them," Wonder Woman explained, moving on. "Like this!"

As she approached several students with her hand outstretched, some ran, others shoved their hands in their pockets, and most just pretended not to see her. Miss

Martian was not one of the lucky ones. Her hand trembled as Wonder Woman took it in hers and began shaking it so vigorously that her head bobbed up and down until she just disappeared. Literally.

"Oops! Where'd she go?" Wonder Woman asked. "Invisibility must be a fun power to have. That reminds me, I have to go, too. It's so nice getting to know you, Supergirl. If you have any questions, just ask. Oh, and please call me Wondy. That's what all my friends call me!"

"Wondy, what does . . . ," Supergirl began. But Wonder Woman had already flown away.

Alone at her locker—a private space on the second tier of storage units, near the ceiling, since she was a flyer—Supergirl wasn't sure what to do. She was relieved when Bumblebee flew up to her. "Everything okay?" she asked just as someone rounded the corner and called out.

"Supergirl, I'm Barbara Gordon. I'm here to give you your locker combination," Barbara said. "I can also help you with any tech concerns."

"It's true," a voice said softly. Supergirl looked around but didn't see anyone. "It's me," Miss Martian said meekly, reappearing in front of her. The shy green girl looked slightly shaken after Wonder Woman's vigorous greeting. "I can read minds. And yes, it's true, everyone here *is* so nice and helpful. Well, *almost* everyone."

Supergirl noticed a girl in a glorious lavender outfit

watching her. *She* didn't look friendly. Miss Martian disappeared once more.

"Ignore Star Sapphire," Bumblebee whispered in her ear. "She's rich and spoiled, so she may not be the best friend in the world."

Supergirl took note of this, but at the same time, reminded herself that with everything that had happened over the past month, she wanted—no, *needed*—to make as many friends as possible. She longed for a lifetime of friends.

"Hello!" Supergirl said, waving.

Star Sapphire gave her an almost imperceptible nod. When the purple ring on her finger glowed, Supergirl found herself feeling happy just to be in Star's presence. But when she turned her back and walked away, Supergirl felt alone once more.

# CHAPTER 6

"Good morning!"

"Good morning!"

"Good morning!" Supergirl made sure to greet everyone she saw with a smile. Maybe they'd want to be friends. One could never have too many friends, right?

"Good morning!"

"Good morning!"

"Good morning!" she said, smiling brightly.

Wonder Woman was at the cereal dispensers, happily filling up several bowls with colorful crunchy-munchy bites. "Join us!" she called out to Supergirl as she headed to her table.

Supergirl looked down at the crispy dark brown pancake and gray-green scrambled eggs on her tray. They reminded her of Aunt Martha's hearty breakfasts, only these had an entirely different color palette. Supergirl smiled at Wonder Woman, grabbed a big bowl, and said, "Be right there!"

If Wonder Woman was a cereal fan, then so was she!

A chic girl with shiny straight black hair removed her sword from an empty chair and scooted over. "You can sit here," she said. She tossed a peeled banana in the air and sliced it so that it covered her waffles, creating the letter *K*.

"I'm Katana."

Supergirl reached out to shake her hand, spilling her bowl of cereal in the process. She watched in horror as bite-sized bits of colorful sugary goodness rolled around on the floor. The crunching could be heard throughout the dining hall as some Supers tried to avoid the mess, while others purposely stomped on it.

Parasite growled and grabbed a broom. His purple skin complemented his blue-gray janitor's uniform. Though he hated cleaning up after the teens, at least it was better than prison, where many of his cronies had ended up.

Wonder Woman gave Supergirl a consoling smile and offered her one of her seven bowls of cereal, which Supergirl accepted with a thank-you.

"Good morning, roomie!" Supergirl called out to Bumblebee. The tiny moons and stars were delicious.

Bumblebee gave her roommate a sleepy nod. They had been up all night. Yesterday, when Bumblebee had generously said, "If you have any questions, just ask!" Supergirl had made a list.

Supergirl looked down at her notebook and was about to continue her questions, when Bumblebee took a big gulp of her honey lemon tea, and said, "Oh! Let's give someone else a chance to answer, shall we?"

"Oh, okay," Supergirl agreed, glancing around the table. Everyone averted their eyes except for Wonder Woman.

"Ask away!" she said. Was she always this nice? Supergirl wondered.

Supergirl: Is there a mascot at Super Hero High?

WW: *Not yet.*

S: Who's the hardest teacher?

WW: *All of them.*

S: What happens when your powers go out of control?

WW: *Happens to all of us. You practice, practice, practice.*

S: Can we get a new student ID if we don't like our photo?

WW: *No, but don't worry. No one looks good in ID photos.*

To prove it, Wonder Woman showed Supergirl her student ID. In it, her eyes were closed. Supergirl tried to stifle a laugh. Katana glanced over and wordlessly whipped out her ID. In the picture she looked like she had just bitten into a lemon. Bumblebee set down her tea and showed hers. Everyone at the table burst out laughing.

"Hmmmm," said Cheetah as she strolled past and glanced at the photos. "Yes, those never come out well, do they?"

Supergirl shook her head, unable to talk since she was laughing so hard. Hers looked the worst—her left eye was half open and her mouth was set in an unattractive grimace.

"Here's mine," Cheetah offered.

There was a stunned silence at the table as everyone

passed around Cheetah's ID. Cheetah shrugged. "What can I say? I was having an off day."

Supergirl handed the ID back to Cheetah. The feline hero's photo looked beautiful. Cheetah's long, thick brown hair was accentuated with an amber swatch that complemented her tanned skin and big brown eyes. Her smile was more of a smirk, but still, she looked fashion-model-ready.

"See you later, ladies," Cheetah purred, tucking her ID into her backpack. Before she left, she pointed to Supergirl's photo. "Looks just like you!" she said.

★

"No, you don't look like a goofy goober," Wonder Woman said as they walked to Intro to Super Suits. Supergirl was still worried about her ID photo. "You look good."

"I do?" Supergirl could feel herself blushing.

"Yes! Well, not your student ID, that looks funny. But I love your costume!" Wonder Woman said.

Supergirl grinned. Coming from Wonder Woman, it was a huge compliment.

Wonder Woman had a great costume—blue pants trimmed with stars and high red boots adorned with wings. Then there was her red top with a gold W that crossed her shoulders— and that tiara with the ruby star nestled into the top of her long, thick black hair . . . wow!

"This class helped me create my costume," Wonder

Woman told her. "If you want to change your look, it can help you, too."

Supergirl hesitated. She thought Wonder Woman liked what she was wearing. But maybe she was wrong—

"Supergirl!" Crazy Quilt called out. Her teacher was wearing a patchwork vest, a poufy purple shirt, and tight, tapered dress pants. "Here, here, come up here. Let's take a look at you!"

Supergirl ran toward the front of the room, but before she got there—"Oomph!"—she knocked over a basket of snapdragon plants sitting at the edge of Poison Ivy's desk. "So sorry!" she said, helping Poison Ivy gather the plants before they bit any students.

"That's okay," Poison Ivy said as her flowing red hair whipped around. She waved her hands in the air and willed the snapping plants back into the basket, securing the white wicker lid.

"Supergirl," Crazy Quilt reminded her. "Here, here. Up front, now."

As Supergirl stood at attention and bit her lip, her teacher critiqued her costume: the short flared red skirt with yellow trim, the top whose blue matched the color of Wonder Woman's pants, the white collar, her short sleeves, and the red high-top sneakers. "Hmmm . . . ," Crazy Quilt said, circling her so many times Supergirl got dizzy. "Hmmm . . . !"

He stood in front of her with his arms crossed, nodding, then shaking his head, then nodding again.

"Yes, yes," Crazy Quilt finally said. "Yes, there is plenty of room for improvement, wouldn't you say? Like that big *S* on your shirt. We can do better than that, can't we?" He looked around the room, nodding at his own suggestion.

Supergirl opened her mouth to speak, but before she could say anything, Crazy Quilt was applauding himself. "Yes! Brilliant! I've got it! I will offer extra credit to the student who supplements your costume to its best advantage!"

"Yes, but I like . . . ," Supergirl tried to say.

"Of course you like my idea," Crazy Quilt said, puffing himself up and tugging at the corners of his vest. "Class, do you like it, too?"

Star Sapphire, Miss Martian, and The Flash agreed. Extra credit was a good thing. A great thing. It could help bring up a grade. At Super Hero High, getting good grades—in addition to defensive fighting and knowledge of the universe—was important.

"Excuse me," Supergirl said, tapping Crazy Quilt on the shoulder. "But this is my family crest, and—"

"Don't worry!" he assured her. Supergirl released a sigh of relief until he said, "We'll make it much better!"

Supergirl felt her throat tighten. She didn't want it to be better. She loved her family crest. She was proud of it. In fact, she loved her entire costume. Her mother had made it for her. But before Supergirl could say anything more, Crazy Quilt was barking out the details of his extra-credit assignment as the class immediately got to work.

# CHAPTER 7

**W**ildcat looked up from his clipboard. Phys ed had just started. "I've heard good things about you, Supergirl," he growled. "Now we'll see if what they're saying is true."

"What are they saying?" Supergirl asked, curious. Who was talking about her? Did someone say something bad?

"That you're the strongest girl in the world," Cheetah said, whispering in her ear. "But if that's true, you're going to have to prove it."

Supergirl smiled at her classmate. She sensed that Cheetah didn't like her, but she didn't know why. Supergirl made a mental note to be extra nice to her.

"Let's do this!" Wildcat yelled. He watched without comment as Supergirl ran through a battery of tests. Lifting weights, then cars, then boulders. Stopping rockets midair. After each test, Supergirl tried to gauge his response, but Wildcat just nodded and scratched numbers down on his clipboard.

Finally, Wildcat spoke up. "Class," he said. His deep gravelly voice commanded attention. This was the teacher who had coached the Super Hero High team to victory in the recent 100th Super Triathlon. Supergirl knew all about it, and him, from watching Harley's videos.

"Class," Wildcat said again. "I've double-checked the numbers, and though this is just a preliminary test, it looks like Super Hero High may be home to the most powerful teen in the world!"

"Wonder Woman!" Supergirl found herself saying out loud. Wondy was great at everything.

"Supergirl!" Wildcat corrected her. "But don't get too cocky. We won't know for sure until we get to the real tests."

Supergirl saw Principal Waller nod to him from the back of the room before continuing on her way.

Wonder Woman looked stricken. Then she took a deep breath and with determination strode toward Supergirl. Holding her head high, Wonder Woman was the first to congratulate her. "That is so awesome, Supergirl," Wondy said, shaking her hand. "Well deserved."

"But, but . . . I thought you were the one . . . ," Supergirl stammered.

Wonder Woman shrugged. "It was me. But there are enough powers to go around. Anyway, the stronger *you* are, the stronger *we* are."

Cheetah approached the two of them and stretched out. "This test doesn't count. It wasn't an official one. Plus, your powers mean nothing if you can't control them."

"Ignore her," Katana jumped in. "I do."

As Cheetah and Katana glared at each other, Harley Quinn pushed them apart and shoved a camera in Supergirl's face. "Supergirl, we now know you have super-duper strength. But what's your weakness? Everyone's got one. Mine's potato chips." She paused to laugh at her own joke. "Hey, Supergirl, is it true that Kryptonite is yours?" Harley turned the camera on herself and shouted, "My 'Harley's Quinntessentials' viewers want to know!" before turning it back on Supergirl.

"I guess so?" Supergirl said so only Harley could hear her.

"What's that? Really?" Harley said to the camera, her eyes widening. "Well, sorry, 'Quinntessentials' viewers, but that's need-to-know information. I need to know it, but you don't!"

Katana whispered to Supergirl, "Don't give away all your secrets; they can be used against you. Like saying that Kryptonite is your weakness. Harley covered for you this time, but next time you may not be so lucky."

Supergirl nodded appreciatively.

What she didn't add was that she felt like she had a lot of weaknesses. Unlike the rest of the Supers, who appeared to be so confident, there was so much she couldn't do yet. Supergirl hoped that no one would find out.

★

"I've tried everything and can't get this to work," Supergirl admitted to Barbara Gordon.

"Let me take a look." Commissioner Gordon's daughter examined the computer. In addition to overseeing the police department, her father had taken on a part-time job teaching at Super Hero High. "What seems to be the problem?"

*My parents are gone,* Supergirl thought. *My planet exploded. My teacher wants me to change my costume, and I can't control my powers—and that's just for starters.*

"I'm trying to send an email to my aunt Martha and uncle Jonathan," Supergirl explained, pushing her bangs aside. "But my computer keeps shutting down."

Barbara pressed a button and the recruitment video for Korugar Academy came up on-screen. The view count from Supergirl's computer numbered seventeen. "Someone's interested in Korugar," Barbara quipped.

Supergirl blushed bright red. "It's just that . . . well, despite the strength tests, I still don't feel like I'm in the same league as the rest of the Supers. My powers are all over the place!"

Supergirl clamped her hands over her mouth. "Oh, wow," she exclaimed, embarrassed. "Please ignore everything you just heard, okay?"

Barbara closed the back of the computer. She put down the small screwdriver she'd been using. "I'm honored that you confided in me," she said, taking off her glasses. Her green-gray eyes looked friendly. "Don't worry, I won't tell anyone. In fact, I can help," she offered. "I can use my technology to create a battery of tests to chart your progress, giving you exercises and critiques along the way." Barbara paused. Now it was her turn to look embarrassed. "That is, of course, if you'd like my help."

"You would do that for me?" Supergirl sputtered.

"Of course," Barbara said. "That's what friends do for each other. Oh, and you can call me Babs if you want. Harley started that nickname, and it looks like it stuck."

Supergirl felt warm inside. Her first real friend on Earth and she couldn't have asked for a nicer one. She stood up and gave Barbara a huge hug. "I would LOVE your help," she said. "THANK YOU! I'm so happy you go to Super Hero High, too!"

"Uh, I go to Gotham High. I just work here," Babs corrected her. "Would you mind releasing me?" she said, trying to breathe through Supergirl's crushing embrace. "The first thing you have to learn is just how strong you are."

"Sorry, I've only had my superpowers since I've been on Earth, and that's really only been a few weeks," Supergirl said apologetically.

"I know," Babs said. "That's not a long time. Just remember: to be your best you need to employ your superpowers, brainpower, *and* willpower. Do you think you can do that?"

"Yes," Supergirl said, nodding. "Superpower, brainpower, and willpower!"

★

When not working with Barbara, Supergirl went into overdrive in her effort to make new friends. Luckily, she was very friendly. But despite her best efforts, she was also still *super* accident prone, always tripping over her untied shoelaces, flying too high too fast, misjudging her strength. When Supergirl let Cheetah cut in the cafeteria line, she bumped into Cyborg, sending him skidding across the room. When she carried Star Sapphire's science project for her, Supergirl crushed the mini volcano, causing hot lava to spill all over Frost and flooding the hallway with steam. And when she flew up to get *Astrophysics* and *Astro Modern Monuments* from a high shelf for Miss Martian, Supergirl toppled the bookcase, causing a domino effect that practically decimated the library.

"Oh! So sorry! I'll put everything back," she told the stunned librarian. "I promise."

★

It was hard starting at any new school. But starting at Super Hero High, where the standards were out of this world, *and* starting midterm, when classes were in full swing, Supergirl soon found herself falling behind.

"This doesn't look good," Principal Waller said, putting down her glasses. She had been reading a progress report. "Supergirl, I don't want you to stress out about your grades; however, I won't lie. They're important."

Supergirl nodded. She thought about Korugar Academy, with no tests and no grades and no pressure to succeed— or at least, that was how their brochure made it seem. On Krypton, she had been one of the top students. But then, her former high school wasn't full of overachieving super heroes.

"I've assigned tutors for you," Waller said. "Wonder Woman will help you with Weaponomics. Harley will be with you in phys ed. Poison Ivy will be your partner in science, and Hawkgirl will cover Super Heroes Throughout History. For Flyers' Ed, there's Bumblebee. And in Intro to Super Suits, you'll be with Katana."

Supergirl felt a wave of relief rush over her. Help was on the way!

# CHAPTER 8

As the days marched on, Supergirl felt more confident about her studies. Her tutors were totally great—well, Katana wasn't always very patient when it came to cutting cloth for Intro to Super Suits. Often, she'd throw bolts of cloth in the air and slice them into patterns before they hit the ground. Then there was science, when sometimes Poison Ivy was so enthusiastic that she'd skip over the basics and blow up the room—although she was always overly contrite when this happened. In Flyers' Ed, Bumblebee seemed to forget that Supergirl was new to flying and would want her to perform seemingly impossible formations alongside her.

When Hawkgirl tutored Supergirl in Super Heroes Throughout History, she was a stickler for details, expecting her to have memorized even the footnotes, leaving Supergirl thoroughly befuddled. Plus, Harley was always bouncing around, videotaping Supergirl chewing her pencil or twirling her hair when she was confused, which was often. But other than that, everything was going great!

"Excuse me, Mr. Fox. Why is it I'm in this class? I don't have any weapons," Supergirl asked one day.

Lucius Fox, in his wool suit and crisply cut vest, dressed more like a Wall Street banker than a Weaponomics instructor. "Great question!" he said, straightening his bow tie. "Who here sports weapons?"

Katana raised her sword in the air, and several other students brandished their weapons proudly.

"Who here comes into contact with weapons?" Every single student raised their hand. Mr. Fox nodded. "This class also teaches you how to deflect the weapons that may be used against you. For example, Supergirl, Kryptonite is your weakness, correct?"

"Yes," Supergirl replied. Though she hadn't experienced the effects of the green glowing radioactive element firsthand, the Kents had warned her that it could drain her of her strength. It could even kill her if she stayed in contact with it too long.

"We don't have a quick antidote yet for your body's response to Kryptonite," Mr. Fox continued. "But we can make you aware of the threat and how to avoid it."

Supergirl took notes. Of course! A weapon could be a tool—or a danger, depending whose hands it was in. She was learning so much—and moments of understanding like this made everything going on in her life make more sense. Yet everything in her life *still* seemed so overwhelming. Was that normal?

"Barbara? Barbara Gordon, where are you?" Mr. Fox called out.

Barbara stepped out from behind the door. "Ah, there you are. Have you been here the whole time?" he asked. She nodded, almost sheepishly. Supergirl had noticed that Barbara was often hanging around during class. "Listen up, Supers!" Mr. Fox continued as he strolled up and down between the desks. "Barbara will be conducting a weapons check, making sure they all work properly. Hand them over."

"Supergirl," Barbara asked. "Will you help me log them in?"

"Sure!" Supergirl leapt up and began collecting the weapons with such enthusiasm that a few of them accidentally smashed a window. The good news was that Mr. Fox was able to use Supergirl's stumbles as the starting point in a lecture about weapons safety. While Supergirl smiled through his talk, inside she was mortified to have let Barbara and Mr. Fox down.

★

By the time Intro to Super Suits rolled around, Supergirl's stomach was in a knot. Crazy Quilt was pacing the runway, excited to see what his students had come up with for the SECA—Supergirl Extra Credit Assignment.

As each student gave her an item to add to her costume, or showed a sketch of what they thought she should wear, Supergirl did her best to appear pleased. Some designs were conservative—like Hawkgirl's, which was nearly identical to the gray suit jacket that Waller wore. Others were over-the-top, like Harley's. Harley had added horns and firecrackers to Supergirl's costume. Some looked practical—like a skirt-of-many-pockets that The Flash had created. And still others were fashionable without function—like the fabulosity of Star Sapphire's full-on sparkly ball gown and matching gem-encrusted high-heeled shoes, which would have made her look like a super pop star.

As the anxious students awaited the decision, each hoping to earn the SECA, Supergirl's stomach began to cramp with stress. She wanted to please everyone. But how could she? And what was worse, she wasn't even sure any of the costume changes were right for her.

"It's time. Is everyone ready? I'm ready! Tell us!" Crazy Quilt said, opening his arms and holding them up toward the sky. He paused for a moment for dramatic effect. "Who will be awarded the extra credit? Who among us will add to Supergirl's iconic costume? This costume will inform the world of who Supergirl is, where she's been, and where she's going. This costume, like all of yours, is her calling card!"

There was a discernible shift in the room as the Supers sat up straight, admiring their own costumes. Then all eyes turned as Supergirl approached the front of the room slowly, her usual enthusiasm dampened with dread. The silence at first appeared to be calculated to ramp up suspense, but it soon turned to awkwardness. Supers glanced around at one another in confusion.

Crazy Quilt leaned into Supergirl. "Everyone is waiting," he reminded her. She nodded, knowing that she had to say something soon.

Finally Supergirl began haltingly, "I love what everyone's done." Cheetah and Star Sapphire gave each other knowing grins. Hawkgirl and Poison Ivy looked serious. Katana looked confident. Harley winked at Supergirl, then focused her camera on her.

"Come on, tell us!" Crazy Quilt cut in, eager to hear the decision. "Who gets the SECA—Supergirl Extra Credit Assignment? SECA! SECA! SECA!" he began to chant, pleased with the sound of his own voice.

"Well, um. No one," Supergirl said in barely a whisper.

No one in the class moved.

Crazy Quilt shook his head. "No, no, no, no, that's not how it works, Supergirl," he gently reminded her. "You pick one design and the student who created it gets the SECA. And as we all know, Crazy Quilt is quite generous with his extra credit!"

Supergirl lowered her head. "I love and appreciate what everyone's done," she said to the silent room. "I really, really do. But my costume, the one I showed up in, the one I'm wearing right now, is something I don't want to change. At all."

"You could have a change for the better," Cheetah muttered under her breath. "Your costume is so boringly normal."

"You see . . ." Supergirl struggled to explain, absent-mindedly fiddling with her crystal necklace. "My mom made my costume. We worked on it together." Supergirl took off her cape and showed the class the small white tag on the inside that read MADE BY KARA AND ALURA.

Supergirl put her cape back on and continued, her voice getting stronger. "Red was Mom's favorite color, hence my red skirt. The royal blue is Dad's favorite, that's why my shirt is blue. I like yellow—that's on the trim. See here? The cape is like the one my dad had when he was a boy." Supergirl took a breath. "The crest, this big S-shape, has been in my family for generations. And as for my red high-top sneakers, well, I just think they look cool.

"As Crazy Quilt said," Supergirl continued, her voice getting even stronger, "our costumes tell the world who we are, where we've been, and where we are going. My name is Kara Zor-El, only child of Zor-El and Alura. My planet and everyone on it, including my parents, were destroyed. What I'm wearing honors my parents and my planet. This is who I was and still am."

Supergirl turned to Crazy Quilt. "Please don't make me change," she begged.

Crazy Quilt was sobbing, along with half the class. He produced a handkerchief from inside his sleeve and loudly blew his nose into it. "Dear, dear child," he said, taking her hands in his, "your costume is perfect just as it is." Several classmates nodded. Harley was crying so hard she could hardly hold up her video camera. "You wear your costume with pride, and as for the SECA, one hundred percent of the extra credit goes to . . . you."

After consoling Crazy Quilt, Supergirl turned and faced the class. "I want to share the extra credit with my classmates who worked so hard on my behalf, and divide it equally among them. May I?"

Her teacher nodded and burst out crying again as he answered, "Yes, Supergirl! Yes! Super idea!"

# CHAPTER 9

Supergirl had a single blue notebook, albeit a big one, for all her classes. She was sitting in her Super Heroes Throughout History class and had just opened to a clean page when Liberty Belle announced, "I have a fun project for all of you. You'll be working on your family histories. We'll unveil them on Parents' Night."

A buzz of excitement filled the room. So many of the Supers had rich histories to fall back on. After all, this high school counted many of the most famous super heroes in the universe as alumni, and a great deal of the students were legacies, having had relatives who had gone to the school before them. Still, there were a fair amount of students who didn't have any super heroes in their lineage—but were about to create a legacy of their own and make their families proud.

If only her parents could see how far she'd come, Supergirl thought. But she gave herself only a few seconds to think about this. She never wanted to be a downer, so she made it a point to be extra cheerful, always ready with a smile, a word of encouragement, or a joke or two. Wonder Woman was always telling people, "That Supergirl fits right in here! She makes me happy just to be around her!"

Supergirl liked hearing that. It felt so good to have friends. When she was with others, there was no time to be anything but cheerful and busy.

However, as cheerful as Supergirl was during the day—raising her hand in class, helping others, joking about her inability to control her new powers—when the sun set and the stars came out, it was an entirely different story.

Nights were hard. When she was alone in bed with the lights out, Kara thought about her parents, her friends, and the life she left behind when Krypton was destroyed.

Sometimes she'd have nightmares about it, waking up and crying out in her sleep, frightening Bumblebee. Other times, Kara would dream that she was having supper with her mother and father and they were talking about the vacation they were planning to take to Wonderful World, the new family theme planet two solar systems over. Kara didn't know which was worse: the nightmares that startled her awake in a cold sweat, or the dreams that broke her heart when she awoke to find out they weren't real.

★

The Knitting and Hitting Club was quite popular, though sometimes it got out of hand, resulting in knitting needles being confiscated and students being sent to detention. Yet no one could deny that the colorful blankets, sweaters, and whatnots that the club members knit, when they weren't practicing hitting each other, were quite spectacular.

Supergirl signed up for the club with all good intentions. Katana, who had a keen eye for cutting-edge design, had talked her into it. "You can be totally creative here!" she enthused. "Look at this!" Katana unfurled a sleek coat with matching boots, hat, and sword-carrying case she had knit out of gray steel wool and rare yellow-hued Yeti yarn.

As the days at Super Hero High wore on, Supergirl had time to reflect on all that Martha and Jonathan Kent had done for her—taking her in, caring for her when she was at her most vulnerable. Had she even thanked them? The least she could do, she thought, was knit them a present. However, during the first Knitting and Hitting meeting, Supergirl not only managed to unravel a giant ball of yarn, she also got several club members tangled up in it as well. It took the school's Booby Trap Disposal Club, aka Anti-Evil Engineering Society, to sort everyone out. Though the AEES Supers were adept when working with bombs and other incendiary devices, they had never dealt with yarn before. Once everyone got sorted out, Supergirl apologized profusely, then went right back to work. Her goal was to have the present ready to give to her aunt and uncle on Parents'

Night—that is, if they showed up. Technically, they weren't her parents.

Later, Supergirl sat on her bed and examined her knitting. It looked more like knotting, she thought as she turned the colorful blob of yarn this way and that. It was so tangled she couldn't even find the knitting needles.

There was a knock on the door. "Someone request tech services?" Barbara asked, stepping inside.

Supergirl put her knitting down. "I was trying to send my aunt and uncle a weekly update, but I crashed the computer." Barbara waited for Supergirl to humbly add, "Again."

Tech was not Supergirl's strong suit. Luckily, it was something Babs excelled in.

Without even looking, Babs retrieved her tools from her Utility Belt. With the skill of a master surgeon, she began adjusting this and that, and saying mysterious things that sounded like, "Hmmm, looks like a diffused dialectic electric gigabyte whatchamacallit 4.0."

Supergirl liked having Babs nearby. The two had been honing Supergirl's superpowers in secret. With Barbara's analytical abilities, she was able to set up a regime to help Supergirl learn to control her powers. And while Supergirl had improved almost 74.3 percent in strength and stalwartness, and her flying was nearly under control, she had more progress to make with aim, accuracy, and not tripping over her own feet.

"Babs," Supergirl ventured, "can I ask you something?"

"Sure," Barbara said as she finished up. To make sure the computer was running properly, she logged onto "Harley's Quinntessentials." On the screen they could see Harley interviewing Miss Martian, who kept answering Harley's questions before she asked them.

"What was it you wanted to ask me?" Barbara said, shutting off the "Quinntessentials" channel. The room was suddenly, blissfully, silent.

Supergirl had made many new super hero friends. She was still in awe of Wonder Woman—who wasn't? Hawkgirl was nice, but such a rule follower that every time Supergirl messed up, which was often, she was afraid that Hawkgirl might report her. Harley was—well, Harley—busy creating her broadcast empire. Katana was great, if sometimes a bit too honest and blunt. Bumblebee was the sweetest roommate ever, never complaining about Supergirl's nightmares. And while many underestimated her, Poison Ivy was so talented, but a full-on introvert. However, it was Barbara Gordon, who wasn't a super hero and didn't even attend Super Hero High, whom Supergirl felt closest to.

"I . . . don't really know what a super hero is supposed to do," Supergirl confessed.

When Babs didn't answer right away, Supergirl was afraid she was going to get laughed at. But instead, Barbara said, "Maybe we should go old-school for this question."

Supergirl wasn't sure what that meant, but she didn't want to admit it. Barbara Gordon was the smartest person she had ever met. If anyone knew what she was talking about, it was her.

"Follow me," Barbara said, already out the door.

As they made their way down the empty hallways, Supergirl thought she saw a roundish green creature scampering around a corner. She almost said something to Babs, but instead she kept going, certain she must have been seeing things. *Leftover nightmares,* Supergirl thought.

Just as they neared the library, a terrifying shadow towered on the wall—this one too large to ignore. When it spoke, both girls jumped back.

"What do you want?"

*CRASH!*

Supergirl and Barbara were startled by the sound of glass breaking.

"Help me!" someone cried.

Supergirl searched the hallway with her super-vision and spotted a figure stepping out of the darkness. The old lady was nowhere near as big as the shadow she had cast.

"My heart!" she said, clutching her chest and staggering. "Mercy me, you girls really scared me."

"I'm so sorry, Granny Goodness," Barbara said, hastily picking up the old woman's cane and handing it to her.

Supergirl recognized the elderly librarian. She had met her before when she'd knocked down most of the bookshelves.

"Let me help you," Supergirl said, extending her arm and supporting Granny Goodness as they walked into the library.

"My, but you're strong, Supergirl," Granny Goodness noted.

"You know who I am?" Supergirl asked, surprised.

"Yes, of course!" Granny Goodness's voice was warm and friendly. "I've been following your progress . . . since you helped rearrange my library earlier. You've been doing a good job, dear. You're well on your way."

*On my way where?* Supergirl wondered as she helped Granny Goodness ease into a chair.

"We're here to find books on being a super hero," Barbara explained. "Stuff that may not be on the Internet. Book books, like with paper pages. Old historical tomes, that sort of thing."

"Books that smell like books," Supergirl said helpfully.

"I can certainly help you with that," Granny Goodness assured them.

As she tottered up and down the aisles, the librarian used her cane to inch books off the top shelves and then toss them to the girls. Babs was carrying an impossibly tall stack, and Supergirl had a stack twice as tall—in each arm.

"I think this is enough for now," Barbara said as her books swayed precariously.

"More than enough, thank you," added Supergirl. She wondered how she'd ever have time to read all of them.

"Wait, don't go yet!" Granny Goodness insisted. She reached into her cookie jar and pulled out two cookies. She popped one into each of the girls' mouths.

Supergirl smiled as she chewed. The cookies reminded her of home. Her father was famous for his sugar cookies dusted with starlight. He always set aside a batch and hand lettered a fancy *K* in blue frosting for *Kara.*

"Come back anytime," Granny Goodness said, lowering her voice and adding, "Nighttime is especially good; that's when I get lonely." Supergirl nodded. She knew how that felt. "And please," the old lady added, "call me Granny."

# CHAPTER 10

Barbara looked at her watch. "Oh no!" she moaned as they headed back to the dorm. "My dad is going to be so mad at me. I'm late, I gotta go!"

"Thanks for taking me to the library," Supergirl said, and scooped up the books her friend was carrying. "I'll see you tomorrow!"

Supergirl continued on alone. She was fairly certain she knew the way back, but with the books blocking her view, she hit a wall and backed up. The door in front of her was made of steel and above it was a small sign that read:

BOOM TUBES

DO NOT ENTER—THAT MEANS YOU!

Supergirl had heard of the Boom Tubes. They were supposed to take you somewhere, but she was hazy on the details. Maybe, she thought, they could take her back to the girls' dormitory! Babs had confided that she had discovered all sorts of secret passageways at Super Hero High. Supergirl set the books down and tried the door. It appeared to be stuck, so she tried it again, this time with more force.

Oops.

Supergirl stared at the door handle that had come off in her hand. Her confusion was broken by a loud siren and blinking red and yellow lights.

Panic!

"WHAT ARE YOU DOING HERE AT THIS HOUR?" a voice boomed.

Double panic!!

"Uh, I—I'm lost," Supergirl sputtered. "I was just trying to find my way back to the dorm. I was at the library. I was . . . I was . . ."

Waller looked at the piles of books around Supergirl. "You weren't trying to access the Boom Tubes?" she accused, crossing her arms and narrowing her eyes on the handle in Supergirl's grip.

Triple panic!!!

"I don't even know what a Boom Tube is," Supergirl admitted as the alarm continued to scream. Clumsily, she tried to put the handle back on the door. "I was just trying to get back to my room, honest!" Her voice started to crack. "I'm so sorry for setting off the alarm." Her shoulders slumped. "I'm not doing so well as a super hero, so I was doing some extra research," she tried to explain.

"You're doing fine," Waller said with a sigh as she turned the alarm off. The lights stopped flashing and the air was filled with a sudden silence. "The Boom Tubes can take you anywhere. But they've been off limits for years. No one, I repeat, *no one* has permission to use them."

"They can take you anywhere . . . ?" Supergirl asked as she scrambled to pick up the books.

Waller nodded. "Anywhere."

At that moment Supergirl felt like a failure for breaking the door handle, setting off the alarm, and incurring the wrath of Waller. She wondered if the Boom Tubes could take her to Korugar Academy. If only she knew how they worked.

"You sure ask a lot of questions," Principal Waller said. Supergirl froze. "That's a good thing," the principal assured her. "You don't pretend to know everything, like some of the other students. The Boom Tubes are teleportation devices. Since you came mid-semester, you missed my All-Access All-School Tour. But I'll fill you in on it now."

"Teleportation devices?" Supergirl said.

"Yes, they can take you anywhere in the universe you want to go," Waller repeated.

Supergirl's heart skipped a beat. "Can they take me back to Krypton to see my parents?"

The Wall shook her head sympathetically. "No, it's not a time machine."

Supergirl swallowed her sadness. "Oh, okay. Teleporter, not time machine. I get it now. Principal Waller, everyone here knows so much more than I do," she confessed. "I don't think I'll ever catch up."

As Waller stared unblinkingly at her, Supergirl fidgeted. Was she in trouble? Would she be expelled? It was hard to tell what the principal was thinking. Even Miss Martian said that she could never read Principal Waller's mind. Maybe Korugar Academy *would* take her, Supergirl ventured. She really didn't have anywhere else to go. She wasn't even sure if the Kents wanted her on the farm—after all, they'd seemed eager to send her away to Super Hero High.

"Supergirl," Principal Waller finally said. "You are here because of your potential. Because of what you are capable of becoming." She paused. "I'm going to show you something no student at Super Hero High has seen. I think you have the maturity to handle it. Are you ready?"

Relief! Supergirl nodded. "I'm ready!" she said, curious as to what was in store.

Waller scanned her credentals on the reader next to the sealed Boom Tube door. A red glow appeared at the security check panel, followed by a low buzz. Silently the double-reinforced unbreakable steel door opened to reveal a large sealed-off room with what looked like portraits lining the walls.

These were the legendary Boom Tubes—the teleportation devices that could take you anywhere in the universe!

Through the round portals, Supergirl gaped at Skartaris, the world at the center of the Earth where a young apatosaurus nibbled on some tree leaves and then happily burped. In Atlantis, the fabled sunken city, it looked like renovations were being completed on an underwater castle. Over in Florida, a rowdy group of retirees were arguing over bingo. And in Korugar, home to the Yellow Lantern Corps, Supergirl could see Korugar Academy students milling around a classroom taking selfies, drinking milk shakes, and passing notes.

"At Super Hero High, you're learning how to be a super hero—not just for Metropolis or Earth, but for the entire universe and beyond," The Wall said.

Supergirl couldn't look away from the portals. So much was happening everywhere. "Why aren't the Boom Tubes used all the time?" she asked, mesmerized. "This is amazing."

"The Boom Tubes can be dangerous in the wrong hands. Sneak attacks, deceptions. Look here." The principal walked her over to a portal on the far side of the room.

Supergirl's eyes grew big as she stared at the fiery, desolate landscape of Apokolips. Fierce female warriors were sparring as coaches yelled instructions. None wore the safety equipment Super Hero High students were required to use when training. No one looked happy.

"What are they preparing for?" Supergirl asked, flinching at the hostility on their faces.

"Years ago," Waller began grimly, "Darkseid, the ruler of Apokolips, hijacked our tubes and brought his army to

Earth. Our super heroes nearly lost the battle against his evil." She ushered Supergirl out of the Boom Tubes door, shut it, sealed it, reattached the door handle, and reset the security system. "It's rumored that one day his Female Furies—the girls you saw sparring—will try to take over Earth once more. That's why the Boom Tubes must remain sealed off," Waller cautioned. "It's for the safety of Super Hero High and the world."

# CHAPTER 11

Even though she was supposed to be focusing on her classes, Supergirl's mind kept wandering back to the Boom Tubes. So when she overheard the members of the Junior Detective Society talking about them, she couldn't help listening in.

"Hi!" she said, chasing them down the hallway. "Um, Boom Tubes? What's up with that?"

The Flash looked at her, then glanced at Bumblebee.

"Oh, nothing," Bumblebee said, trying to sound sweetly nonchalant. "We're just strolling along, minding our own business. La, la, la . . . nothing's happening."

Supergirl wondered if that was a hint that she was supposed to be minding her own business.

"Don't you have your Knitting and Hitting Club now?" Hawkgirl asked pointedly.

"I suppose I do," Supergirl said. She wished that the Junior Detective Society members would include her.

Of all the clubs on campus, they had a reputation for actually getting stuff done and providing a service to the school. Unlike the Eponymous Epicurean Elites Club, where the members just sat around and ate fancy desserts, or the Mediation and Meditation Club, where members argued, then napped, Waller actually counted on the Junior Detective Society. And that made their standards a little higher than some of the other school clubs. They wanted new members to prove that they had sleuthing chops.

"Okay, see you all later," Supergirl said reluctantly. She knew when she wasn't wanted. As she began to walk away, she looked down and noticed something on the floor. "Wait!" she said, picking it up. "Could this be a clue?"

Supergirl held up a leaf.

This time the members of the Junior Detective Society took her seriously. Hawkgirl used tweezers to carefully place the leaf in a plastic bag, then labeled it.

"It'll take some time, but I'll run some horticultural tests to analyze it," Poison Ivy said, taking possession of the evidence.

"This could be the clue we've been looking for!" The Flash declared to Hawkgirl and Poison Ivy.

As the trio walked away, chattering enthusiastically, Supergirl stood alone.

"Supergirl?" The Flash called back to her.

"Yes?"

"Good job!" he said.

"Yes, good job," Bumblebee and Hawkgirl chimed in. "We'll let you know if this leads anywhere."

Supergirl felt warm inside. Maybe she *wasn't* so out of place here after all.

# PART TWO

# CHAPTER 12

That night, like the one before it, and the one before that, Supergirl couldn't sleep. This time, though, she quietly slipped out of her room so as not to wake Bumblebee, and grabbed her knitting on the way out. The stars were shining and the moon was full when Supergirl flew up to the top of the Amethyst Tower that had so warmly welcomed her a couple of months earlier. There, she resumed knitting her present for the Kents. She thought about what her life would have been like if her planet had not exploded. She missed her mom and dad.

As Supergirl looked toward the night sky, she imagined the stars realigning and creating a new constellation—one that featured her mother and her father, both with their arms around her. Her parents were smiling like they had been in the family portrait that once hung in their living quarters. Kara smiled back at them, for a moment refusing to believe that nothing existed of her former home planet. Nothing but memories.

As magically as the constellation had appeared, it slowly faded away into darkness. Kara muffled a cry and set down her knitting needles. All her parents had ever wanted was for her to be happy. She felt like she was letting them down.

★

Supergirl was surprised to wake up in her bed tangled in her sheets. The last thing she recalled was sitting alone on top of the Amethyst Tower missing her former life. The knitting lay on a nearby chair, still incomplete.

"Hurry or you'll be late for breakfast," Bumblebee warned on her way out. "It's Waffle Wednesday, and Beast Boy has challenged Katana to another eating contest!"

Supergirl used her super-speed to get ready for school. She was exhausted, having stayed up most of the night, and put her high-tops on the wrong feet, causing her to trip more than normal.

"Sorry."

"Sorry."

"Sorry," she said as she bumped into her classmates. Some laughed. (It was especially funny when Supergirl crashed into people.) But others were growing weary of her clumsiness. At least they could see Wonder Woman's enthusiastic, bone-crushing handshakes coming. With Supergirl, one could never tell when she might trip, fall, or fly into them.

It seemed like she had just sat down to breakfast when someone began poking her.

*Huh?*

Supergirl sat up.

"You just face-planted into your waffles," Hawkgirl said as she peeled a piece of waffle off Supergirl's face. The sticky syrup remained, and when Supergirl tried to wipe it off, a corner of white paper napkin stuck to her forehead.

"I'm awake!" she announced, a little too brightly. "I'M AWAKE!!!"

No one heard her. They were too busy rooting for Katana and Beast Boy, who were plowing through the towering stacks of waffles in front of them.

Supergirl shut her eyes again. She had a headache. Her super-hearing was going haywire. Through the cheers, she could hear snippets of conversations around the heavy wooden tables that anchored the dining hall.

"This is going to look incredible in fast motion," Harley boasted.

"My phone is broken!" Cheetah complained.

"Have a great day," Barbara said to her father. Supergirl hoped to take a class from Commissioner Gordon next semester. That is, if she could get through this one. "I have to go," Babs was saying as she held on to a computer. "Vice Principal Grodd needs this fixed so he can log all the unexcused absences this month."

"Barbara," her father said, sounding serious. "I am so proud of you. I don't know how you do it. I have problems just turning on my computer—and here you are with a job as tech whiz to one of the most famous high schools in the universe!"

This made Supergirl smile—she loved that Barbara and her father were so close. She leaned in their direction to hear more.

". . . and I can't tell you how relieved I am that you're not one of these Super Hero High kids. Oh, don't get me wrong, these teens are amazing. But with *your* talent and brains, you could rule the high-tech world! Plus, that's so much safer," he added, chuckling. "Barbara Gordon, a super hero? Not on my watch—it's too dangerous for my little girl!"

"I'm not a little girl." Barbara spoke so softly that Supergirl could barely hear her. She accessed her super-hearing, but it wasn't necessary. "Yeah, me a super hero? Never in a million years," Barbara said loudly, laughing along with him. When Commissioner Gordon moved to give his daughter a hug, Supergirl could see her pulling away. "Dad!" Barbara complained. "We've talked about this. No hugging in public!"

Supergirl returned to her waffles. They were cold. She would do anything for a hug from her father.

The center of the room rocked with wild cheers. Katana had bested Beast Boy, having devoured twelve stacks of waffles to his eleven. Both looked ill as they congratulated each other and then ran out of the dining hall clutching their stomachs.

Janitor Parasite sighed. He picked up a mop and followed them.

After Commissioner Gordon bid his daughter goodbye, Cheetah spoke up. Apparently Supergirl wasn't the only one who had heard their conversation.

"It's a good thing you aren't a student here at Super Hero High," Cheetah said to Barbara. "You have zero powers."

Undaunted, Babs motioned to Harley, Catwoman, and Bumblebee, who were making their way toward her. "They weren't born with superpowers, and look how well they're all doing here."

"Yes, but . . . ," Cheetah began. She shut her mouth when the trio surrounded her.

"What are we talking about?" Harley asked, turning on her camera.

"Nothing," Barbara said cheerfully. "Cheetah was just asking me to fix her phone." She picked up Grodd's computer. "Bring it by my IT annex anytime," she told Cheetah. "I'd be happy to look at it. I'll even lend you one of my phones if you need one!"

What the others didn't notice—but Supergirl did—was that when Barbara walked away, her smile faded. She looked as sad as Supergirl felt.

# CHAPTER 13

Supergirl ran after Barbara. About to call out to her, she spied her friend slipping into a broom closet at the far end of the hallway—the one filled with Parasite's cleaning supplies. Huh? It didn't make sense. Supergirl could see a red laser emitting its bright light from a panel. Babs stood still as it scanned her. "B.A.T. access granted," a woman's voice said evenly. Another door inside the closet door slid open and Barbara stepped inside, closing the door firmly behind her. Suddenly, Supergirl could see right through the wall. Her X-ray vision was going in and out like her super-hearing.

Supergirl spotted a handwritten sign that read INFORMATION TECHNOLOGY (IT) ANNEX, BARBARA GORDON, PROPRIETOR. Past that was another room whose walls were lined with floor-to-ceiling shelves of neatly cataloged devices and gadgets.

Supergirl couldn't believe it when Babs pushed yet another button and a bank of shelves electronically rotated until they were directly in front of her. The windowless room reminded her of a cave, albeit a super-high-tech one.

Not wanting to spy, but wishing to comfort her friend, Supergirl walked toward the broom closet. Just as she reached the door, the bell rang. Instantly the hall was flooded with boisterous students who swept Supergirl up in their wake and deposited her at Super Heroes Throughout History. Her talk with Barbara would have to wait.

"Your family history reports should also include what it is in your background that makes you uniquely qualified to be a super hero," Liberty Belle instructed.

Supergirl looked at her fellow Supers. Unlike her, they all seemed to fit right in and had everything figured out.

"Any questions?" Liberty Belle asked. Supergirl admired the Liberty Bell emblem that was knit neatly into her sweater. It gave her an idea.

She raised her hand. There was one place that had most of the answers you could ever hope to find. "May I be excused to go to the library to do some research?"

★

As Supergirl made her way past the science lab, the hall monitor stopped her. "I need to see your ID, please," Hawkgirl said.

"You know who I am," Supergirl reminded her.

"Yes, but I'm officially on hall monitor duty and one can never be too safe," Hawkgirl said. She was a stickler for the rules. "ID, please. I need to know you're not a SWAHP."

"A what?" Supergirl said.

"Student Without A Hall Pass," Hawkgirl informed her.

"But it's me!" Supergirl protested.

"There are rules and there are rules, and this is the rule," Hawkgirl said with a stern look.

After being given the official go-ahead to proceed, the young Kryptonian was greeted warmly by Granny Goodness. "I was hoping to see you again," the elderly librarian said. She smelled like freshly baked cookies. "What can I help you find?"

"I'm not really sure," Supergirl said, haltingly.

"Come, come," Granny said. Her sensible rubber-soled shoes matched her sensible short gray hairdo. "Follow me. Let's go into my office."

Well-worn books lined the shelves in Granny's office. Granny settled in behind her messy desk. Next to a cookie jar was a black-and-white photo of an attractive young couple and their twins.

"Your grandchildren?" Supergirl asked, pointing to the children.

Granny Goodness shook her head. "The photo came with the frame," she said, chuckling. "But let's talk about you!"

Munching on a cookie, Supergirl told Granny how she'd ended up at Super Hero High. She could see the old lady's eyes start to well up with tears. "Dear child," Granny said, reaching for a tissue. "We have so much in common. I was an orphan, too."

An orphan? Supergirl had never thought of herself as an orphan. But technically, Granny was right. This made her heart ache even more.

"Unlike you, though," Granny confided, "I came from a poor family, and while many looked down on me, there was one person who looked past my meager upbringing, took me in, and raised me. For that I shall be forever grateful and indebted."

Granny stopped and stood with the aid of her cane. She patted Supergirl's shoulder. "We're two of a kind, Supergirl," she said. "If you need someone to talk to, you know where to find me. Oh, look at the time! You best get back to class, dear. And here, take some of my cookies for yourself and all your friends!"

# CHAPTER 14

Supergirl had reluctantly agreed to meet teen reporter Lois Lane after school. Wonder Woman had assured her that Lois would write a good and fair article about her. "You should see all the stuff she's written about me!" she exclaimed.

Supergirl was too embarrassed to tell Wonder Woman that she already had. It was clear even among all the Supers at school that Wonder Woman was a leader among leaders. She was popular and kindhearted, and nothing seemed to faze her.

Lately, Supergirl was feeling overwhelmed by the sheer number of videos Harley was posting about her—and how many of them included her falls, tumbles, and spills. Never mind that most of them featured her showcasing her super-strength; it was those that made her look silly that she remembered the most.

And why was Supergirl even on the Internet in the first

place? Harley hadn't asked her if she wanted to be. No one had even asked her if she wanted to be a super hero, or if she wanted superpowers. No one had asked her anything.

Still, Supergirl didn't want to make waves. She wanted to make friends. If she didn't, she'd be alone in the world.

And that scared her.

★

As Supergirl flew to the interview, everyone already seemed to know her name. Most people waved or cheerfully shouted to her. Near downtown Metropolis, Supergirl stopped to help a car careening down a steep hill, its brakes having failed. Swiftly, she stopped the car, then carried it to the auto repair shop with the driver leaning out the window taking selfies of the car in flight.

Nearing Centennial Park, Supergirl heard a boy cry, "Save Rainbow!" With care and compassion, she rescued the kitten, who seemed content to stay up in the tree. Later, using her super-vision, she spotted a speeding train about to derail. In a flash, Supergirl bent the steel of the train track back into position and was on her way.

By the time Supergirl landed at Capes & Cowls Café, Lois Lane was already waiting for her inside. Before entering, Supergirl brushed a little dirt from her cape.

"No, really, it's okay that you're late," Lois insisted as Supergirl apologized for the third time. "You were saving people and kittens and trains! That gives me lots to write about."

"Who would want to read about me?" Supergirl asked, genuinely surprised.

"Lots of people," Lois assured her. Supergirl liked that Lois's long, straight hair was no-nonsense, and that she took lots of notes. Her handwriting was neat and confident. Supergirl's parents always used to tell her to slow down when she wrote.

"You have a compelling story, Supergirl," Lois said. "It's like you came out of nowhere. . . ."

"I came from Kryp—" Supergirl started to say before stopping herself. She didn't want Lois to think she was sassy.

"I mean you weren't on anyone's radar," Lois continued. "Then BAM! Suddenly, the strongest teen on Earth shows up. Of course my readers are dying to know about your incredible powers. But I want to write about the *real* you— what makes you tick, what motivates you, what you want to do with your life, what you expect life to offer you. Are you game?"

Supergirl sipped her water, then chewed on an ice cube. That was a lot to ask, and she wasn't sure even she knew the answers.

"Wonder Woman has told me terrific things about you," Supergirl began. "So have a lot of the other Supers. But honestly, I'm not sure I'm ready to be interviewed like that just yet." Supergirl cringed. She hoped Lois wouldn't be mad at her, but she wanted to be honest. "Is that okay?"

Lois closed her reporter's notebook and put down her pen. "Sure, it's okay, Supergirl. I know I ask a lot of questions. It's my job—but more than that, I'm just curious about everything. We can do the interview whenever you're ready. In the meantime, will you let me buy you a smoothie?"

Supergirl exhaled with relief. "Yes, please!" she said. "I'd love that."

Lois waved to someone across the room. "Steve! We're ready to order!" She explained to Supergirl, "Steve Trevor works here—his dad owns this place. We've known each other since we were little. He's a good guy."

A thin boy with a mess of blond hair made his way toward them, expertly weaving through the crowded café. He had a pencil tucked behind his ear, and when he smiled his braces glistened. While he chatted with Lois about a math test, Supergirl glanced around. A couple of girls were playing *Oh, No! Orbit Zone,* the new retro board game, with fierce determination. Over by the window a girl with a guitar was strumming the new interstellar hit "My, My, Oh My Milky Way." And nearby, a round of comet checkers had gotten out of hand when a boy wearing a CAD Academy jacket lit several checkers on fire and hurled them at his opponent.

Supergirl studied the CAD Academy kids. She had heard rumors about that school. According to Katana, it had a disproportionate number of bad eggs and would-be super-villains. Its real name was Carmine Anderson Day School, but most people thought CAD stood for Criminals and Delinquents.

Still, Supergirl felt at home at Capes & Cowls Café. Packed with teens from the local high schools, the restaurant somehow managed to be cozy and hip at the same time. Waller had always insisted that her students get out into the real world as much as possible to meet and mingle with others. "To save the world, you must be a part of it," she'd remind them.

Just then, Wonder Woman rushed in. "Hi!" she said brightly. "How's the interview going?" Her head turned from Supergirl to Lois Lane and then back to Supergirl. "You guys look like you have a secret."

"Not a secret," Lois clarified. "Just nothing to go public with quite yet."

"Oh! Well, snakes and smoothies and strawberry pajama tops," Wonder Woman said, turning all shades of red.

"Are you okay?" Supergirl asked, reaching out to her friend.

Lois tried to stifle a laugh. Steve Trevor was standing at the table, matching Wonder Woman's red coloring as the two stared at each other.

"Shake, rattle, and roller coasters?" he said, not taking his eyes off Wonder Woman.

"I see," Supergirl said, giving Lois a knowing look. On

Krypton, kids had crushes on each other all the time. She had even had her share. "They're both just tongue-tied," she observed.

Lois nodded. "You got that right."

They laughed while Wonder Woman and Steve looked at each other as if no one else was in the room. It was like they had put each other in a trance.

"Order up!" the cook called from behind the counter. "Steve, order up!" he shouted again.

Steve didn't seem to hear him, but Supergirl did. She nudged him, albeit a little too hard, and sent Steve flying toward a trio of CAD Academy kids, knocking over their table and spilling food everywhere. As the angry students closed in around him, Wonder Woman stepped in and broke up the fight before it started. "It was an accident," she said, standing tall, her hand on her Lasso of Truth. Everyone grumbled, but the incident wasn't worth taking on an Amazon.

As everyone in Capes & Cowls talked about what had just happened, Supergirl, turning her own shade of red, made a hasty exit. Flying over Metropolis, she bemoaned the mess she had made of the afternoon.

# CHAPTER 15

That night as she passed Hawkgirl's room, Supergirl could see her sending her nightly email to her grandmother, Abuela Muñoz, in Venezuela. They were extremely close. Supergirl wished she had someone like that in her life.

Sure, she had Aunt Martha and Uncle Jonathan, but whenever she thought about them, she also thought about the circumstances that had brought them all together. Supergirl wished she could reciprocate the love they showed her, but something stopped her. Instead, she sent cheerful, chatty emails telling them about school. Whenever Aunt Martha called her and asked, "How are you doing, Kara?" she'd answer, "Good, just fine," thinking that was what they wanted to hear.

Bumblebee was at her Junior Detective Society meeting when Supergirl sat at her desk and picked up a sketch she'd been working on. She wrinkled her nose. It wasn't great, she thought. Her mother had loved the arts, and the two of them had always enjoyed drawing together. Sometimes, her mom would start a sketch, then pass it to Supergirl, who'd add to it, then pass it back. The drawing would go back and forth until it was done—a piece of art that the two of them had created together, side by side. Many of the sketches had covered the coolbox door in their kitchen on Krypton, alongside numerous candid family photos.

As Supergirl thought about this, a wave of panic washed over her. Her parents! No photos of them remained, she realized. Nothing was left when the planet exploded. What if she forgot what they looked like?

Frantically, Supergirl began to draw. Her mother, her father, the two of them together. Alura and Zor-El. Mom and Dad. More and more sketches, but to her, none of them captured what they truly looked like. Soon her room was littered with paper.

"Hello? I'm not disturbing anything, am I?" Barbara asked. Her eyes dropped to the piles of sketches on the floor.

"Oh . . . um, no . . . ," Supergirl said, gathering up the drawings at super-speed. "I was just—"

Barbara held up her hand. "You don't have to tell me anything," she said. "I'm just here to run the bimonthly anti-evil security checks on everyone's computer." She picked up a wayward sketch. "This looks nice," she said before handing it over. It was a sketch of Supergirl's mother and father, with Kara between them.

"It's not!" Supergirl yelled, tearing the drawing into

several small pieces. "It doesn't look like them."

Babs stepped back. "Whoa . . . I'm sorry if I've upset you."

Supergirl pretended she had something in her eye so Barbara wouldn't see her crying.

"Hey," Barbara said, putting her arm around Supergirl. "Is there something you want to talk about, maybe? Not only am I a tech wizard, but I'm a pretty good listener, too."

Supergirl looked around the room. "I'm scared I won't remember them," she admitted. "My parents. Every day I'm here is a day I've been away from my mom and dad." Her eyes were moist. "Babs, I miss them so much."

Kara held on to the crystal necklace around her neck. It glowed green at her touch.

Barbara nodded and sat down in front of Supergirl's computer, not saying anything. Maybe she hadn't been listening, Supergirl thought. Maybe she was embarrassed by her outburst and ignoring her. It looked like Barbara was getting right back to work installing the anti-evil software. But Supergirl was wrong.

Babs gathered up the sketches and scanned them using a device on her watch. Then she wirelessly uploaded them to the computer. With a couple of keystrokes, she accessed B.A.T.: Super Sketch Artist Pro.

"I created this program for my father's work at the police station," she explained. "It helps the police identify criminals and missing persons." Barbara stopped when she saw the look of shock on Supergirl's face.

"Oh, wow. I'm sorry. I didn't mean to imply that your parents are either of those, but . . ."

Supergirl tried to speak, but nothing came out. Instead, she stared at the screen in awe. A perfect likeness of her parents was looking back at her. Both were smiling and waving to her.

"It's them," she finally managed to say. Her heart was racing. "It's them."

"We need to get to a super-deluxe 7-D printer," Babs said. "Then you can have your own copy to keep."

"There's a printer in the library!" Supergirl said gleefully.

Barbara leapt up and chased her out of the dorms. "Supergirl, wait for me!" she called out.

★

As they raced to the library, the girls passed Beast Boy, who was sitting on top of Amethyst Tower.

"Hello!" he shouted down to them. He was hanging by his tail, having turned into a sloth.

Supergirl tapped into her super-hearing. "I'm practicing being nocturnal," he explained, quite pleased with himself. Within seconds Beast Boy went from a sloth to a porcupine to a cougar to an eastern woolly lemur. Then, as a finale, he turned into a hippo and balanced on one foot on top of the tower.

"Watch out!" Supergirl called, ready to catch him if he fell.

A second before he was about to squash Barbara, Beast Boy turned into a bat and disappeared into the night, laughing.

"Bats," Barbara said to Supergirl. "You gotta love them!" But Supergirl was already hurrying inside the building.

The massive halls were empty as the girls made their way past the Boom Tubes door. In the library, Granny was nowhere to be seen. Babs used her master key to start up the 7-D printer. Soon the mega machine was chugging and whirling. Supergirl stood silently waiting . . . and waiting . . . until finally something rolled out. Gingerly, she picked it up. She was trembling. Then she gasped. In the palm of her hand was a small dimensional hologram of her mother and father smiling at her.

"It's another one of my B.A.T.—Barbara-Assisted Tech—inventions," Barbara said modestly. Then she added, "It's patented."

"Whatever it is, it's beautiful," Supergirl said, choked up. "Thank you, Babs. Thank you soooooo much!"

Barbara hugged her back. "All part of my job," she quipped, adding, "And all part of being your friend. Okay! Look at the time. Supergirl, I need to get back to work if I'm going to get all the anti-evil security checks done by lights-out. See you later!"

Supergirl waved goodbye, her eyes still on the B.A.T. hologram.

"Hi, Mom," she whispered. "Hi, Dad."

"Your parents?" someone asked.

Supergirl whipped around to find Granny Goodness standing behind her.

"Yes," she said proudly.

"I'm sure you miss them terribly," Granny said, offering Supergirl a sugar cookie. "You probably talked to your mom a lot, didn't you?"

Supergirl didn't feel quite right talking about her mother to a stranger. The dark, book-lined room held ominous shadows, and Supergirl's instincts told her that something was wrong. But as she bit into the buttery cookie, she found it harder and harder to resist the charms of the little old librarian. With each bite, Supergirl's reservations began to melt away.

★

Before going to sleep that night, Supergirl put the B.A.T. hologram on the nightstand next to her bed. With her head on her pillow, she stared at her mom and dad. They smiled back at her.

In the dark her crystal cast a soft green light on Kara. Finally, her eyelids fluttered shut and she drifted off into the first solid sleep she'd had since arriving on Earth.

# CHAPTER 16

"**S**ecurity breaches are everywhere on campus!" Bumblebee announced. Though she tried to look worried, her eyes shone with excitement.

"Yes, and encrypted messages are being sent off-Earth," Poison Ivy added as she absentmindedly nibbled on two mini-muffins, one in each hand. "But no one knows what planet they're from!"

Supergirl had just taken a big bite of oatmeal. She wanted to try all the dining hall breakfast foods before deciding which ones were her favorites. So far she hadn't found one. "What's happening?" she asked through a mouthful of mush. She crossed oatmeal off her list.

The Flash pulled up a chair but was too nervous to sit down, so he kept holding it. "Someone or something has been trying to infiltrate Super Hero High!"

"How do you know?" Supergirl said. Would it be wasteful

not to finish the oatmeal? It was like eating a bowl of gooey lumps.

"How do you *not* know?" The Flash shot back.

Supergirl's face heated up. It was true that she had been spending a lot of time knitting and working with Barbara on her powers. Plus, she had been reading oodles of books on super heroes. So many that she could recite the history of the greatest Supers in the universe. But what Supergirl hadn't realized was that with all the studying she'd been doing, she'd been ignoring the super heroes all around her. The ones in training who were alert to the goings-on at Super Hero High.

"Sorry, Supergirl," The Flash said. He finally sat down, folded a slice of toast in two, and shoved it into his mouth. "It's just that the Society has been monitoring this for so long and I'm kinda obsessed with it. I forget that not everyone is as clued in as we are."

"There have been several suspicious attempts to break into the Boom Tubes, and Waller has asked us to monitor them," Bumblebee explained.

"Boom Tubes?" Supergirl said, so startled that she accidentally flung a spoonful of oatmeal across the room. She was mortified when it hit Star Sapphire.

Supergirl had often stopped to look at the steel door, wondering what it would be like if she could travel through the Boom Tubes just once—maybe to check out Korugar

Academy. The tests at Super Hero High were so hard. She wasn't book smart like Hawkgirl, or a scientist like Poison Ivy, or as creative as Katana (though Supergirl excelled in phys ed). The idea of a school without tests continued to appeal to her—though not as much as when she'd first arrived.

"Hey!" Star Sapphire cried, marching up to Supergirl and getting in her face. "Excuse me, Supergirl, but gee, I wonder who's responsible for this." With no lack of drama, Star revealed an unattractive gray lump of oatmeal on her purple top. In a split second Supergirl began to wipe off the offending breakfast food.

"Drop it, Supergirl," Star Sapphire hissed, grabbing her napkin from her. "You've made a big enough mess as it is."

Harley caught it all on video, then turned the camera on herself. "Fashion! Conflict! Cafeteria food!" she reported. "One never knows what they'll encounter at Super Hero High!"

When Supergirl returned to the table, Hawkgirl and Katana had joined the others. All the Supers had their heads together, exchanging rumors and theories about the Boom Tubes and the security breaches.

Supergirl sat back and listened. Topics ranged from a disgruntled ex-student stirring up mischief to an evil warlord from another planet trying to take over the world. Or it could be an elaborate CAD Academy prank—their pride still hadn't recovered from coming in second to Super Hero High in the Super Triathlon. The speculation continued as the group walked out of the dining hall.

As Supergirl headed to Intro to Super Suits with Katana, a warning sounded in the distance. "Boom Tubes access denied! Boom Tubes access denied!"

Just then, someone—or something—sped past them in a blur. It was The Flash! "Let's follow him!" Supergirl cried out.

The Flash stopped at the Boom Tubes door. Hawkgirl and Poison Ivy were already there, talking nonstop. They were examining a cluster of small scratches at the bottom of the door. Supergirl thought she caught a glimpse of something rounding the corner.

"Uh . . . uh . . ."

"What is it?" Katana asked.

Supergirl rubbed her eyes. "I thought I saw a little monster," she said, unsure.

Cheetah strolled past carrying a foam board with a diagram of the major food groups on it. "She'll do anything for attention, won't she?" Cheetah sniped.

"No, really, I saw something," Supergirl insisted. "At least, I think I did. It was little and scary, but also cute and— Oh, I don't know! I didn't get a good look at it, it was going so fast."

Poison Ivy turned back to the Boom Tubes door. "Well, be sure to let us know if you see it again," she said kindly.

Supergirl promised. Then she bent down and picked up something off the floor. "Here," she said, handing the red cloth to Poison Ivy. "You dropped this."

"It's not mine," Poison Ivy said, looking it over. "Flash, is this yours?"

"Not mine," he said, handing it to Hawkgirl.

"Not mine, either," Hawkgirl said, examining the tiny initials sewn into the piece of cloth. "I don't use a handkerchief, and my initials aren't . . . GG."

# CHAPTER 17

As the week wore on, the security breaches sputtered to a stop. Everyone, except for the Junior Detective Society members, chalked the whole thing up to internal malfunctions.

"I think they just want it to be some big spectacle," Cheetah said, looking straight at Harley's video camera as she stood on the stairs. Frost and Star Sapphire stood behind her nodding as Green Lantern and Beast Boy repeatedly photo-bombed the interview.

Supergirl snuck past the commotion and sped toward Waller's office. "Barbara!" she yelled, waving and dodging in and out of the mass of students in the hallway. "Hi, Babs!"

Barbara looked guilty. "Supergirl! Hey, I'm sorry I haven't been around to help you train, but I've been swamped." She lowered her voice. "I've just finished testing the school's breakers, electrical conductors, switches, and power distribution blocks. All are in working order, so that blows the internal malfunction theory."

"Then what is it?" Supergirl asked.

Barbara shook her head. "It's a total mystery. Hey, we should resume your training soon. That is, if you want to."

"Yes, yes, I do!" Supergirl shouted happily. She cleared her throat and dialed down her enthusiasm, not wanting to seem too dorky. "Um, sure. Yes, I'd love for you to help me."

As the two headed outside, Babs adjusted her Utility Belt. There were all sorts of technical-looking tools on it. "We've intercepted a series of cryptic messages from outer space, but so far no one can tell what they say. Could just be a miscalculation in our data gathering, but we need to be safe." She slowed her pace. "It's so odd. I was getting close to determining the origin of the messages, but then they just stopped. I want to keep sleuthing, though."

"I understand," Supergirl said, forcing a smile. "You're busy. Anyone can see that. I don't want to bother you."

Barbara looked hurt. "Yes, I'm busy. But, Supergirl, you're my friend, and I'll always have time for you."

"Really?" Supergirl asked. Her eyes widened and she grinned.

"Really," Barbara assured her. "If I'm neglecting you, you only have to say something. I can't read minds like Miss Martian, you know."

"I knew you'd say that," Supergirl joked.

★

If there was ever a time when Supergirl needed Barbara's help, it was now. In phys ed, she completely overshot the end of the runway. Instead of landing on the giant X with an arrow pointing to it and a sign that shouted STOP HERE!, Supergirl plowed into a group of dignitaries from a visiting planet, sending everyone, including non-flyers, flying.

In Intro to Super Suits, she unfurled a bolt of fabric with too much strength, causing it to completely unspool and trip everyone in its wake. And when she used her heat vision to help Poison Ivy's greenroom experiment, the warmth accelerated the growth of the Villainous Vines, and they attacked the entire science lab, including poor Janitor Parasite, who had just arrived to clean up a spill.

Despite Babs's encouragement, Supergirl was feeling less and less like a future super hero and more like a super failure. Her head knew what to do, but her body and powers wouldn't cooperate! Plus, there was a C-minus that threatened to turn into a D in Super Heroes Throughout History. All because when Raven had joked that the retro assignment, a 1970s report on TV super heroes, was to be done in hieroglyphics, Supergirl had thought she was serious.

As the month came to an end, every time Supergirl walked past the Boom Tubes, she couldn't stop thinking about their potential. Not that she'd ever really use them. But . . . where could they take her? Would it be so bad to slip into Korugar

Academy just to see what it was like? No tests meant no bad grades. Supergirl tried to use her X-ray vision to see past the lead-based metal door, but only succeeded in giving herself a headache.

However, what she could see were the guests outside arriving at Super Hero High. Whether they were driving, flying, or teleporting, they were coming in droves. And they were all headed to something Supergirl had been dreading.

Parents' Night.

# CHAPTER 18

The teachers, Waller, and the students were all on their best behavior, though it was difficult for many, and every now and then someone slipped up majorly. Like Vice Principal Grodd, who carelessly tossed a banana peel on the floor, causing Star Sapphire's mother to teeter off her high heels and slip. Luckily, Hawkgirl was there to fly in and catch her. Then, instead of apologizing, Grodd just wiped his massive brow with his red handkerchief, grunted, and stomped away, knuckles dragging on the ground.

It wasn't just Grodd who messed up. In her enthusiasm, Wonder Woman almost bruised several parents' hands when she shook them. Luckily, Poison Ivy was standing by to whisper, "Easy, go easy," whenever the slightest hint of a grimace was evident. Miss Martian was so overwhelmed by the crowd, she kept turning invisible when anyone spoke to her . . . and so did her sponsor, the Martian Manhunter himself. And when Beast Boy slipped a whoopee cushion onto Commissioner Gordon's chair, Cyborg laughed so hard he nearly popped a screw loose.

Supergirl stood alone in the far corner of the gym watching her peers. Some tried to act cool around their parents. Others, like Bumblebee, wouldn't stop hugging theirs. Supergirl touched her crystal necklace. She recalled her first day of kindergarten on Krypton, when she wouldn't let go of her mother's legs. "Kara, sweetheart." Her mother spoke gently but firmly. "It's time for me to go. Everything will be okay. Always do your best, Kara, and you'll be fine. I promise."

Every year after that, on the first day of school, Supergirl's mother would say the same thing. "Everything will be okay. Always do your best, Kara, and you'll be fine. I promise."

Every year but this one.

Beast Boy and his mentor from the Doom Patrol, The Chief, shared the same spirited sense of humor and were constantly laughing. Abuela Muñoz, video chatting in to Parents' Night, looked like an older, elegant version of Hawkgirl. And then there was Wonder Woman's mother— Queen Hippolyta, ruler of Paradise Island.

Even the other parents—most of whom were super heroes themselves—seemed thrilled to bask in the presence of the Amazon queen, who was as strong as she was beautiful. Supergirl could see where Wonder Woman got her self-assurance, power, and grace. And she couldn't help laughing when her normally serious flight teacher, Red Tornado, raced over to Hippolyta and began babbling and, to everyone's embarrassment, knelt before her.

"Supergirl!" someone yelled.

"Yoo-hoo!" another voice called out.

It was Uncle Jonathan and Aunt Martha! They had told Supergirl they were coming to Parents' Night. Still, she was surprised to see them.

At first, Supergirl thought the Kents looked out of place as the two Midwestern farmers mingled with some of the greatest super heroes in history. Supergirl watched Wonder Woman proudly introduce her mother to everyone. Katana was trying to explain her wild friend, Beast Boy, to her mortal relatives who had journeyed all the way from Tokyo. It didn't help that he kept changing his form, showing off.

As the Kents waved, Supergirl approached them. It would be up to her to make them feel at ease. After all, she knew firsthand how overwhelming this place could be to outsiders. But Supergirl wasn't prepared for what happened next.

Before she made her way across the room, others beat her to them. Everyone already seemed to know Aunt Martha and Uncle Jonathan. They were greeted warmly by students, parents, teachers, and staff.

"How is Superman doing these days?" Harley's father asked as he extended his hand. When Uncle Jonathan shook it and got a small shock from the joy buzzer in his palm, both laughed.

"He's excelling in college," Uncle Jonathan said.

"He's so busy with Semester in Space that we don't know when we'll see him next," Aunt Martha chimed in.

That was when Supergirl remembered that her cousin had attended Super Hero High just a few years before her. Many of the guests already knew the Kents. Instead of mocking her plainspoken non-super hero aunt and uncle, everyone adored them.

"I'm glad you could be here," Supergirl said, relaxing and finally starting to enjoy the evening.

"We wouldn't have missed it," Aunt Martha replied.

"Yes," Uncle Jonathan added. "We're huge fans of Super Hero High. Look at all you kids—you hold the promise of a better world!"

The Supers who had gathered around beamed.

"Please," Aunt Martha said to Hawkgirl and the others, "you're all invited to the Kent farm for Thanksgiving in a couple of weeks."

Someone tapped her on her shoulder. "Supergirl," Liberty Belle said. "Have you shown your aunt and uncle your family history project?"

For a brief moment, Supergirl's heart fell.

Slowly, she walked the Kents over to the displays on the far side of the gym. Trifold foam core boards stood up on tables, each with a family tree and an illustrated history. Katana's had roots in ancient Japan, Hawkgirl's in Venezuela, and Bumblebee's in Brooklyn, New York. When they finally got to the last one, everyone stopped and stared.

Supergirl had done a drawing of the planet Krypton, in addition to her family tree. At the top was a photo of the hologram Barbara had created for her, and above that was a photo of Supergirl with the caption THE LAST LEAF ON THE TREE.

A poem accompanied the family tree. It read in part:

> *Krypton was my planet*
> *Krypton was my home*
> *Something happened*
> *Something terrible and sad*
> *Krypton was my planet*
> *Krypton was my home*
> *It is gone now*
> *My planet*
> *My family*
> *My home*

Aunt Martha dried her tears and moved to hug Supergirl. "It's just a poem," Supergirl said dismissively, stepping away from her. "It doesn't mean anything."

Supergirl was glad she wasn't tangled up in Wonder Woman's Lasso of Truth.

"Your parents would be proud," Uncle Jonathan said. For the first time, Supergirl noticed the wrinkles etched in his brow.

Before the tears began to fall, Supergirl lowered her head.

She could feel the Kents' warm embrace, yet she couldn't bring herself to hug them back. They weren't her parents. They weren't even her real aunt and uncle. They'd adopted her because her parents had died. They could never replace her mother and father. No one could.

It was a relief when Supergirl heard Waller announce, "Will everyone please move to the auditorium so we can start our formal part of Parents' Night!"

"I'll be right there," Supergirl told the Kents. "There's something I have to do first."

As everyone filtered out, Kara stared at her family tree with her parents' portrait on top.

"They look like you."

Supergirl was surprised to find Liberty Belle standing behind her.

"Missing them?" Liberty asked.

Supergirl nodded, her throat choked up and her stomach in knots.

"I know it must be hard," her teacher said. There was kindness in her voice, not sympathy. "Here at Super Hero High, so many have lost loved ones. That's one reason we do family trees. To remember and honor those we have lost. And to inspire us all to move forward."

Supergirl remained silent, afraid that if she spoke, she might lose it.

"You're doing really well, Supergirl," Liberty Belle assured her. "Super Hero High is here for you."

Before she left, Liberty Belle turned around. "Oh! I almost forgot. Granny Goodness asked me to give these to you. What a sweet little old lady she is!"

She slipped a napkin full of cookies into Supergirl's hand. "I hope you don't mind I had one," Liberty Belle said. "I just can't resist those cookies. No one can!"

★

Faster than a speeding bullet, Thanksgiving week appeared. There was general cheer around Super Hero High, midterms having just ended, so everyone could enjoy the holiday.

Supergirl was doing better in her classes, and had managed to bring up her grade in Super Heroes Throughout History, thanks to her family tree project. She was doing well in Intro to Super Suits, partly due to the extra credit Crazy Quilt had bestowed. Though teachers weren't supposed to play favorites, every time Crazy Quilt saw Supergirl, he would declare in a loud stage whisper, "Perfect. Perfect-o. Perfection. Your costume. Strength. Vulnerability. Hope. Courage. Colors." Then he would strike a pose like the Statue of Liberty or Rodin's *The Thinker.*

It embarrassed Supergirl to have such attention lavished on her. On Krypton she was just a regular girl. "I don't know what to say when people compliment me like that," she confessed to Barbara.

Barbara looked up from the tiny homing device prototype she was building for Mr. Fox. If she was successful, he wanted every student to have one. "Why don't you say thank you?" she suggested.

Supergirl looked at her friend with admiration. Why hadn't she thought of that?

★

Most of the Supers were headed home for Thanksgiving, but not all. "Please," Supergirl told them. "My aunt and uncle say there's plenty to eat and it would make them happy if you joined us." She was working on telling people how she actually felt. "It would make me happy, too," she added.

# CHAPTER 19

"**W**e're here!" Supergirl called out eagerly. The Kent home was quiet. "Hello? Aunt Martha? Uncle Jonathan?"

Aunt Martha came out of the kitchen looking frazzled. "Supergirl . . . Oh! Supergirl! It's Thanksgiving!" She looked surprised.

"Yes, that's why we're here," Supergirl said, peering into the kitchen. It didn't look like anything was on the stove. Hawkgirl and Katana glanced at each other. Beast Boy studied his shoes, and Harley put down her camera.

"Mercy me!" Aunt Martha said, plopping herself down on the couch. "Uncle Jonathan has been sick. Nothing too serious, just a nasty cold he can't shake." Supergirl glanced at the piles of tissues all over the house and leading up the stairs. "But that's meant that all the farming and household chores have all been left up to me," Aunt Martha explained. "I've got all the fixings for Thanksgiving dinner, but I haven't started cooking, and that usually takes a whole day itself."

"Why don't we help you?" Wonder Woman offered, motioning to the other Supers.

Supergirl wished she had thought of that. Wonder Woman always knew what to do.

"I'm great at slicing and dicing," Katana said, brandishing two swords.

"I always cooked at my *abuela*'s side," Hawkgirl said.

"I'm great at eating," Beast Boy bragged. He rubbed his stomach as if to prove it.

"And I'm fast," Supergirl said, trying to think of something to add.

Aunt Martha smiled. "Well, it looks like we'll have a Thanksgiving feast after all!" She paused, then looked out the window toward the crops. "Oh, but there's so much to be done on the farm first. Some of the horses have strayed, and the cows need milking, and, well, I've totally fallen behind."

"We can help with that, too," Supergirl said as the rest of the Supers nodded and Harley picked up her camera again.

"Let's get to work, then," Aunt Martha said.

Beast Boy turned into a border collie and herded the horses out of a ravine where they had gotten trapped. Supergirl carried them to safety.

Using her blades, Katana approached the wheat field, reaping as she sped across it, followed closely by Hawkgirl, who used her wings like a combine machine, threshing and winnowing the stalks, efficiently separating the chaff from the grain.

Meanwhile, with the horses safe, Beast Boy and Supergirl joined Wonder Woman, who was now gathering a bounty of sweet corn, snap beans, tomatoes, and broccoli. Not to mention piles of pumpkins.

"My, my, look at all this!" Aunt Martha said, clasping her hands together when the teens returned. She had been bustling around the kitchen putting the turkey in the oven and getting the fixings ready for pies and mashed potatoes and gravy and . . .

"Oh dear," she cried. "I forgot to get cranberry sauce!"

"Not a problem," Supergirl assured her. "I'll be right back."

After a minute or two, Supergirl returned with several jars of cranberry sauce from Tiptree, England, along with some spiced bread pudding. Then she ran outside to help Wonder Woman, who was talking to the cows. Supergirl showed her how to milk them, then churned the butter and gathered some eggs.

Everyone had a hand in cooking, meaning that the kitchen was a mess. Six super hero teens in one small space, tossing ingredients to each other, shucking corn, and mashing potatoes.

"Cyborg, would you mind turning on the oven and putting the turkey and the pies in?" Aunt Martha asked as she wiped her hands on her apron.

"What? Yeah, sure!" Cyborg exclaimed, just as Harley

threw another egg at him. Both burst out laughing as he tried to bat it back at her.

Despite the chaos, Supergirl noticed that Aunt Martha seemed to be having a great time with her friends. Even she was covered in flour by the time everything was simmering on the stove.

With the turkey in the oven, Wonder Woman suggested they do more chores while Aunt Martha rested. Wonder Woman had never been to a farm before and was enchanted by it. Beast Boy suggested painting the old barn, and Katana picked the colors: red, blue, and gold, the colors of Super Hero High's logo.

Overachievers that they were, not only did the Supers paint the barn in a fetching modern pattern, but when they finished and there was extra paint . . . well . . . it didn't exactly go to waste. Beast Boy pretended he was going to splash Katana, but she kicked a can up in the air and speared it with her sword, and blue paint poured all over his head.

"How about some gold highlights in your hair?" Beast Boy asked, laughing as he turned into a squirrel and, using his tail, gave her gold streaks.

Not to be left out, Harley took out her mallet and pounded two paint cans, causing a splash of color to drench Wonder Woman, who in turn, yelled, "So this is how you paint in Kansas? I love it!"

Wondy lassoed a can of red, then flung it at Supergirl,

who caught it midair and tossed it to Hawkgirl. Hawkgirl caught the can with one hand and set it down. "There's more work to be done," she reminded everyone.

Next up: stacking bales of hay. Hawkgirl and Wonder Woman each stacked towers of hay so high they almost touched the clouds. And of course, Harley captured everything on tape for her Super Super Thanksgiving Special.

As the Supers gathered in the dining room, Uncle Jonathan slowly made his way downstairs. "Would you look at this!" He beamed.

"Uncle Jonathan, you're well enough to join us!" Supergirl said, leaping up to help him over to the table.

Just as he sat down, Aunt Martha came out of the kitchen looking distressed. "I'm so sorry," she said, wringing her hands on her apron. "Everything is ready except the turkey and the pies. The oven wasn't turned on!"

Cyborg's face turned almost as red as his glowing bionic eye. "Uh . . . um . . . er . . ."

"Spit it out," Harley said, aiming her camera at him.

Cyborg looked down at his shoes and said in a barely audible voice, "It's my fault. I forgot to turn the oven on." He glanced up at Harley. "But it's your fault, too! You threw an egg at me!"

They glared at each other.

Supergirl set down her glass of warm apple cider and stepped between them. Then she opened the oven and peered inside. Sure enough, the turkey was as pale as a polar bear—but not for long.

"I got this!" she said. She focused on the bird and, using her heat vision, cooked the turkey to golden brown perfection. Lightly crisp on the outside, juicy and flavorful on the inside.

Next, she turned her heat vision on the pies. Soon the buttery baked scent of golden flaky crust and cinnamon spiced pumpkin and apple wafted through the kitchen. Aunt Martha clapped and gave Supergirl a giant hug.

"Let the feast begin!" Harley shouted.

The mood was jovial, and the food was especially delicious, having been made with friendship and love. Later, as the pies were being sliced, each person around the table said what they were thankful for.

Harley was thankful for her new video equipment.

Beast Boy was thankful for his ability to morph into animals.

Katana was thankful for her ancestry.

Hawkgirl was thankful for her grandmother.

Wonder Woman was thankful for Super Hero High.

Uncle Jonathan was thankful for Aunt Martha, Superman, and Supergirl.

Aunt Martha was thankful for Uncle Jonathan, Superman, and Supergirl.

"I'm thankful for all of you," Supergirl said, motioning

around the table. "And . . . wait!" she cried, racing out of the room. She returned with a fuzzy colorful something overflowing in her arms. Bits of fuzzy yarn stuck out at odd angles. "This is for you," she told the Kents. "I knit it myself."

The Kents smiled at the strange tapestry of colored yarn, not really sure what it was supposed to be. But it was wonderful to them all the same.

"We love it!" Uncle Jonathan gushed.

"LOVE it!" Aunt Martha echoed.

"Group hug!" Wonder Woman shouted.

Surrounded by friends and family, Supergirl's necklace glowed bright as it lit up her face with a joy she hadn't felt since first arriving on Earth.

# CHAPTER 20

The happiness Supergirl experienced at the farm lingered. Anytime she thought about it, her crystal glowed. Still, there were moments when Supergirl feared that it betrayed her parents to be too happy. She was conflicted in so many ways. And when it came to Super Hero High, she wondered if one could feel like they belonged, and at the same time feel like an outsider. Some things were really starting to click into place, like her friendships, and she was doing well in her classes. Supergirl felt great about that. But would everything ever really fall into place? She hoped so, but still she was wary. After all, she'd learned the hard way that nothing was for certain.

"Hmmm . . . you're doing well," Barbara said, studying her charts. She had about two dozen of them on her minicomputer. Each one analyzed Supergirl's progress in different areas: Speed, Flight, Vision (X-ray, Telescopic, Microscopic, and Heat), Hearing, and Strength.

"Let's test your speed on foot again," Barbara said. It was after school, and they were sharing the track with the cross-country runners, who were warming up.

Supergirl shook herself out of her Krypton-infused daydream. She'd been thinking about home again, and how her father always used to bake cookies.

Supergirl stood on her mark. When she heard the tiny click of Barbara's stopwatch, she took off, lapping the members of the Super Hero High track team three times before tripping over her shoelaces and tumbling awkwardly in front of Jay Garrick, the track coach and the original Flash!

"Anytime you want to join the team, you're in," he told her as she leapt up and pretended that nothing had happened. "But you'll need better shoes."

Supergirl looked down at her red high-tops. They were just fine, she noted. Except that the laces were undone, again.

"I'm not surprised he said that," Barbara said, entering the stats into her computer. "Thanks to my B.A.T., my computer can analyze hard data. But even so, sometimes human observations can be telling, too. Coach Garrick's pretty wise." A graph with an icon of Supergirl running came up. "Your shoelaces caused you to trip. All the serious runners wear air-coiled jet sneakers that wrap around their feet like a lightweight shell," Barbara noted. "It doesn't matter how cool your high-tops are if you can't keep them tied."

She motioned for Supergirl to come closer. Her normally optimistic face looked deadly serious. "I want you to remember this," she said, lowering her voice. Supergirl braced herself.

"Double knots," Barbara said.

"Double knots," Supergirl repeated.

Next up was Flight. Supergirl soared majestically around the tall buildings of Metropolis, waving to people as they called out, "Hi, Supergirl!" She stopped in front of an apartment window where a little girl and her brother were playing super hero, wearing towels as capes and jumping off the couch. When they saw her, they raced to the window and blew kisses. Supergirl did a flip in the air, then gave them a thumbs-up before heading to the mountains.

Using her super-hearing, she heard Barbara say, "You're tracking well, Supergirl. All looks great! Do a couple laps around the mountain range, making sure you maneuver through the canyons, then head back in."

Just as she finished her second lap, Supergirl thought she caught sight of Bigfoot, the mysterious creature known for his stealth and his ability to confuse the public. She swooped down to get a closer look, and as Bigfoot ran from her, Supergirl slammed into a tree, causing a chain reaction—tree after tree fell in turn as she watched, horrified.

"Thanks, Supergirl," a logger called out as the toppling trees slowed to a stop. "We were just about to cut them down!"

Supergirl gave him a weak smile and sighed with relief. "I . . . uh . . . meant to do that."

"Well, you have room for improvement," Barbara said kindly when Supergirl returned. "You need to pay more attention to what you're doing and where you're going."

The tests continued, some with better results than others. Finally, Babs said, "Okay, one more. Hearing. Let's see if you've mastered this. Hone into the library and tell me what you hear there."

Supergirl scrunched up her nose. This always seemed to help her hearing. Then she concentrated. She heard rumors and gossip in the corridors, Mr. Fox and Grodd exchanging baked broccoli casserole recipes in the teachers' lounge, and finally Supergirl clued in to Granny's voice. "Someone's been removing books from the library!" the librarian said.

Supergirl could make out Hawkgirl asking, "Isn't that what they're supposed to do?"

"Not without checking them out first." Granny sounded sad.

"Don't worry, Granny Goodness," Poison Ivy jumped in. "The Junior Detective Society is on the case!"

Supergirl listened as Granny thanked them profusely. She could hear the Supers still talking and munching on cookies as they made their way out of the library.

"This will take forever," The Flash said. "If we track down each book on this massive list she gave us, we won't have time for anything else!"

"We're the Junior Detective Society," Poison Ivy reminded him. "We're here to help anyone who needs sleuthing."

"Look," Hawkgirl said. "The Boom Tubes."

"The door looks secure," The Flash noted. Supergirl could hear him knocking. "Anyone home?" he joked.

"Come on," Hawkgirl said, sighing. "We've got work to do and no time to play with the Boom Tubes."

The Boom Tubes. How many times had Supergirl let her mind wander and thought about them? Especially when she did something embarrassing. Like the time Wonder Woman let her try on her tiara and in her enthusiasm, Supergirl bent it out of shape. Or the time in phys ed when she and Green Lantern were in charge of collecting the speedballs and she tossed them too hard, sending him flying across the room. Though everyone applauded, and Green Lantern pretended he'd done it on purpose, he avoided her for days.

Then there was Cheetah and her crew. Even though her teachers seemed to like it when students asked a lot of questions, not everyone else did. Cheetah would growl things under her breath like, "You know you don't get extra credit for hearing yourself talk, right?"

Frost got chilly whenever Supergirl broke a school record in phys ed. Supergirl couldn't understand it. She thought they were all supposed to support and encourage one another. So it was a relief when Frost pulled her aside one day and said, "You missed Super Heroes Throughout History when you took Wildcat's Official Super-Strength Test— Oh, and congrats on the being-the-strongest-teen-in-the-world thing, by the way. Anyway, just thought you'd like to know that Liberty Belle assigned us the universe for homework."

"The entire universe?" Supergirl gasped, unable to hide her surprise. They had just finished covering the world, and she thought the solar system was next.

"Yes," Frost said as Raven stood behind her nodding. "We're supposed to do an illustrated history of the entire universe. Due tomorrow."

The next day, when a weary Supergirl handed in 147 pages of her "Illustrated History of the Universe," an astonished Liberty Belle said, "Great job, Supergirl, but I didn't assign this."

Supergirl was having trouble keeping her eyes open. "But I thought—"

"But it's marvelous!" Liberty Belle exclaimed, looking at the pictures. "I'm going to post these on the bulletin boards and give you extra credit!"

Supergirl smiled, then stopped when she saw Frost glaring at her. Now what had she done?

Later, during lunch, Cheetah strolled over to her. "Say, Supergirl," she said, "I don't think you've even taken part in the new student initiation, and it's overdue."

"What is it?" Supergirl asked, setting down her iced tea.

"Well, in order to show your allegiance to Super Hero High, you're required to dress like a chicken and cluck loudly around the dining hall. Think you could do that tonight at dinner?"

Supergirl nodded. It would be hard to scare up a chicken

costume by then, but if that was what it took to be initiated into Super Hero High, that was what she would do. Right after school, instead of going to her Knitting and Hitting Club meeting, Supergirl flew to the Kent family farm.

"What a wonderful surprise!" Aunt Martha said as she brushed down the horses. "Uncle Jonathan is in the cornfield if you want to say hello to him."

"I can't stay long," Supergirl said apologetically. "I just need to gather some chicken feathers."

Aunt Martha pointed. "There are plenty of loose ones in the henhouse," she said.

That evening, when Supergirl strutted into the dining hall, most students were already seated and eating. She cleared her throat until she got everyone's attention. "Good evening!" she called out in a strong, clear voice. "I'm Supergirl, and I'm a super chicken, and *cluck, cluck, cluck,* I'm new to Super Hero High! *Cluck, cluck, cluck, cluck!*"

There was an uncomfortable silence.

Supergirl could see Cheetah, Frost, and Sapphire trying not to crack up. A feeling of shame washed over her. Had they played a joke on her?

*"Cluck . . . cluck,"* she said weakly. *"Cluck?"*

Laughter started from Cheetah's table and made its way around the room. Supergirl stood frozen in her handmade chicken costume. She could feel her face get hot as the laughter began to turn into a roar. Suddenly, above it all, she heard, *"CLUCK, CLUCK!"*

Looking around as the *"CLUCK, CLUCK"* got louder, Supergirl spotted Beast Boy standing on a chair.

*"Cluck, cluck,"* he called out before turning into a giant chicken. He chicken-walked over to her and whispered, "Dance!"

Dance? Supergirl didn't know any dances. Wait. She knew one . . . Uncle Jonathan had taught her the chicken dance, a silly dance he'd do when they fed the chickens.

Supergirl took a deep breath and yelled, "Chicken dance, everyone!" Soon, led by Beast Boy and Supergirl, everyone in the dining hall, including Parasite and some of the servers, were clucking in a long line up and down the rows of tables.

When they were done, everyone cheered and broke out in applause! Well, not everyone. Cheetah, Frost, and Star Sapphire, who had chosen to sit out the dance, did not look happy.

That night, Harley was in heaven. "Look!" she said to Supergirl. "The dance has gone viral! The president is even considering making it the national dance of America!"

Sure enough, all of the USA and beyond was doing the chicken dance. Supergirl smiled. Now if only the rest of her time at Super Hero High could be as successful.

**N**ights were still hard when Supergirl was alone with her memories. Sometimes she'd have nightmares of cute little green monsters scampering around, or planets exploding. Morning couldn't come fast enough.

When the sunlight finally peered through her window to awaken her, Supergirl smiled. Its warmth felt like a hug as it gave her strength and renewed her spirit to face the day. She made it her mission to brighten up and be as helpful as possible to as many people, animals, and aliens as she could. This included Granny, who, once she was taught the proper steps, excelled at doing the chicken dance, albeit with the help of her cane.

"So," Granny Goodness said after she finished clucking. She sat behind her crowded desk as Supergirl sank into a couch so plush that she felt like she was being wrapped in clouds. "You've two more strength tests coming up. Are you ready?"

Supergirl shook her head. Sure, she'd been working with Babs, and that had been going sort of well. But something always messed her up in the end.

"Maybe I need new shoes or something," Supergirl said meekly, recalling what Coach Garrick had told her. "I know I'm strong enough, and fast enough. But I don't think I'm good enough."

Granny absentmindedly toyed with a snow globe of the solar system, shaking it up so all the planets had unaligned. "I think it's all in your mind, Supergirl," she said thoughtfully.

"What do you mean?"

"I mean," Granny explained, "you're talented enough and have what it takes, but the thing that's stopping you is *you*. Perhaps there are things that are bothering you?"

Supergirl thought about this. Could Granny be right? No, she decided. She was just a mess. No one would argue with that. But then again, all those nights staying up, worrying about things she couldn't control . . . things she couldn't forget. Principal Waller had set up several sessions with Dr. Arkham, the school counselor, when she'd first arrived. And Wonder Woman had said that he was great and had helped her. But Supergirl just couldn't bring herself to talk to a stranger about her deepest, darkest fears and worries.

"Cookie?" Granny asked, shaking Supergirl out of her thoughts.

★

Strength Test Day. Though Supergirl had done massive testing with Wildcat when she first started Super Hero High, this was the official standardized exam. Every school in the galaxy was taking it on the same day. All students were given the same tests, and the scores were tallied, tabulated, recorded, parsed, and examined. Human, alien, animal, mutant, other—everyone was on edge. Your strength standings said a lot about who you were, especially if you were a super hero.

At Super Hero High, Wonder Woman was up first. Supergirl noticed that she didn't look nervous at all. In fact, not only did Wonder Woman look calm and confident, she looked like she was having fun. Supergirl watched her closely for clues on what to do.

In the Creative Strength Category, also known as CSC, students were charged with coming up with something unique. "For my CSC, I'm asking the assistance of a special guest," Wonder Woman said, smiling. "Beast Boy, will you join me?"

"Would I? Oh man, I'm there!" Beast Boy said, leaping up and taking a deep bow. "It's Beast Boy! I'm Beast Boy! He's Beast Boy!" he chanted. The Riddler and Catwoman shook their heads disdainfully.

Wonder Woman whispered something to him and his grin widened. "Sure thing, Wondy. You got it!" he said. In the time it took for him to finish his sentence, Beast Boy had turned into an elephant, but not just any elephant.

A rare jumbo jumbo super jumbo elephant so big that several Supers had to back up to give him room.

With ease, Wonder Woman lifted Beast Boy the elephant over her head, tossing him in the air, catching him, and throwing him higher each time. While the class applauded politely and Supergirl cheered loudly, Wildcat looked on. Supergirl could hear him saying, "Ah, the old jumbo jumbo super jumbo elephant trick. When will I see something new?"

"Thank you, Wonder Woman. Beast Boy, please assume your normal state," the coach said, as both Wonder Woman and Beast Boy bowed to the students and sat down.

Students demonstrated their strengths—some stopping rockets, others bending metal, and still others doing the traditional lifting of multiple thousand-pound weights— while Supergirl thought of what she would do. Encouraged by Wonder Woman, when her name was called, Supergirl raced to the front of the room, ready to ace the CSC.

"Beast Boy," she called out. "Will you join me up here?"

Pretending to be shy, Beast Boy stood up and mouthed, "Me?" Then, pointing to himself, he said, "Ladies, take note of Mr. Popularity."

Supergirl whispered something in his ear. "Heck, yeah!" Beast Boy exclaimed.

"Let's see what you've got," Wildcat said. He was tired and cranky. This was the last strength test of a long day.

Beast Boy shut his eyes, puffed out his cheeks, and morphed into several extinct, and very awkward, creatures before finally appearing as a massive brachiosaur. The class cheered wildly, along with Wildcat, who had instantly perked up. This was something new! Even Wonder Woman was smiling and giving Supergirl an approving nod.

Supergirl approached Beast Boy Dino. Everyone laughed good-naturedly as she walked around him, trying to figure out how to pick him up. Finally, she squatted down and lifted him from his belly, being careful to balance his ginormous frame. Then, slowly, Supergirl lifted him above her head with both arms stretched skyward. The cheers could be heard all the way to Waller's office.

But wait! There was more. Supergirl was now lifting Beast Boy Dino with one arm . . . then one hand . . . and then, could it be? No, maybe people were seeing things, but yes! She was balancing him on one finger . . . her pinky finger!

Harley was going bonkers capturing it all for "Harley's Quinntessentials." "WOWZA! This is gonna break the Internet," she shouted. "I predict a million views a minute!"

To Harley's delight, Supergirl wasn't done yet. Slowly, she lifted herself off the ground and flew above her classmates, with Beast Boy Dino still balanced on her little finger.

Wildcat called out a warning. "Supergirl, be careful! I think you've proven yourself."

Supergirl couldn't hear him, instead focusing on the cheers from her classmates. Buoyed by their encouragement, she was determined to really give them a show—something to remember her by. Taking in a deep breath, she began to zip across the sky still holding Beast Boy Dino aloft on her pinky. Students all across Super Hero High stopped to look out their classroom windows to witness the spectacle. But then, when Supergirl passed the Deadly Double Dutch willow trees Bumblebee had just planted, Beast Boy Dino's nose began to twitch . . .

Supergirl felt his sneeze coming on and then . . . *ACHOO!!!* Before she could say "Excuse you," Beast Boy Dino began to topple and plummet to the ground!

Just before he was about to crush Miss Martian, Wonder Woman bulleted into the sky and caught him, giving him a chance to morph into a tiny bird. He let out a squeaky sneeze and flew away, embarrassed. Beast Boy landed on his feet and hopped away to catch his breath and recover while Supergirl skidded into Wildcat, knocking him over.

"Supergirl," he growled. "Your antics put everyone in danger. That's not what we do here. You'd better learn to control your powers before an innocent person gets hurt!"

Supergirl hung her head. Cheetah purred. Harley got it all on video.

# CHAPTER 22

**S**ure enough, the video of Supergirl dropping Beast Boy Dino broke viewing records. Harley was ecstatic. "Thanks, Supergirl," she gushed, doing a triple backflip. "My ratings are sky-high! You're the best!"

Supergirl didn't feel the best. She felt the worst. Even worse than the worst. The worst-est. Was that even a word? If it wasn't, it should be, Supergirl thought. Maybe in the dictionary it could say "worst-est" and have her photo next to it.

"Are you okay?" Barbara asked. "Um, I saw the video on 'Harley's Quinntessentials.'"

Supergirl didn't feel like smiling, but she did anyway. "I'm fine! I feel great! Everyone makes mistakes, right? And did you see Wondy? Wow! She really saved the day when she caught Beast Boy Dino before he crushed Miss Martian."

"You have a great attitude. I like that about you," Barbara said as she pored over Supergirl's strength charts. "Say, do you know that you got a D-minus on the strength test?"

Supergirl nodded. She knew, and so did the rest of the school. It was times like these that she wished Super Hero High were more like Korugar Academy, with no tests, no pressure, no "Harley's Quinntessentials." There was enough talk of her mess-up everywhere else.

On the ever-popular *Super Hero Hotline* TV show, which spotlighted all the super hero and super-villain gossip, the host patted her tall orange hair and leaned into the camera, whispering, "Is Supergirl all washed up?"

Before she finished winking, her cohost twirled the tips of his impressive mustache and in a faux whisper said, "I won't name names, but people are wondering about her. She came out of nowhere, and suddenly she's supposed to be the most powerful teen in the world?" He wagged his finger. "I don't think so!"

"But she did popularize the chicken dance!" the woman added.

Both hosts leapt up and began dancing and clucking right into the commercial break.

"Well, let's get to work," Babs said, as she switched off the two dancing TV hosts on her phone. Supergirl nodded with relief. "I want you to practice your midair stops and starts," Barbara was saying. "Your climbing could use some work, too. Try this," she continued, scaling up a rock wall in record time.

For a non-Super, Barbara had some serious skills.

"Babs, I don't feel well," Supergirl said, honestly. "Do you mind if we skip training today?"

Barbara looked surprised. "Oh, okay. Sure, no problem. I hope you feel better soon."

"Little chance of that," Supergirl muttered.

"What was that?" Barbara asked.

"I said, I'm sure I will," she said, giving her friend a small smile. "I gotta go. See you later."

★

That week, Supergirl barely muddled through her classes. When her teachers asked, "Any questions?" everyone waited for Supergirl to say something. But she didn't. It seemed like the entire world and beyond had seen Harley's video of Supergirl's airborne disaster, and that, of course, included the student body of Super Hero High. Supergirl watched from the old bell tower as teens congratulated Wonder Woman on her spectacular save.

*PLOP!*

The kindly cafeteria lady ladled some unidentifiable food onto Supergirl's plate. Normally, she would ask how it was made and compliment the chef. But not today. Today she kept her head down, hoping no one would notice her. She even wore a disguise, albeit not a very good one—a baseball cap with her blond hair tucked under it, a blanket draped over her shoulders as a toga, and dark sunglasses.

Supergirl picked up her tray and headed to the far corner of the dining hall. Looking down at her lunch, she recalled Aunt Martha's amazing meals. She wondered if the Kents had seen the video of her epic fail. Probably not. They could barely figure out how to set their electronic alarm clock . . . good thing for roosters.

As she pushed her food around her plate, Supergirl's ear began to itch. She scratched it and heard snippets of conversations around the room. Cheetah was saying, "Who is that Barbara Gordon girl anyway? She's hanging around the school so much, if you didn't know better you'd think she goes here."

At another table, Bumblebee and Hawkgirl gathered around The Flash, who was showing them something on his tablet and saying, "Too many things are going wrong . . . I think Super Hero High may be a target . . . valuable books are still going missing . . . but no time to . . . and now, three weeks later, the Boom Tubes security breaches have started again."

Near one of the five emergency exits, Katana was saying to Miss Martian, "This is not criticism, but maybe you should go invisible a little bit less often. Hey! Where'd you go?"

Supergirl was surprised that she didn't hear anyone talking about her.

Without warning, a loud buzzing filled the air, threatening to burst Supergirl's eardrums. She silenced her super-hearing.

"ALERT! ALERT!" the PA system boomed. "This is not a

test. Super Hero High is on ALERT. Everyone report to the auditorium immediately."

In less than a half second the dining hall was empty, and in two seconds, everyone was seated in the auditorium. Principal Waller stood onstage with her hands behind her back, looking serious as she paced.

"Students, as some of you may already know, there has been an increase in suspicious activity here at Super Hero High," Waller said. Supergirl observed the Junior Detective Society members nodding grimly. "We have reason to believe that an outside force is trying to infiltrate our school. That's why we'll be on Level Seven Alert—Level Ten being the highest—until notified otherwise."

There was a discernible shift in the room. Level 7 Alert! Though few would admit it, most students at Super Hero High were anxious to try out their powers in real life. Enough of this testing and practice stuff—bring on the super-villains!

Supergirl peered over the top of her sunglasses. With the school on alert she felt silly sitting in the auditorium wearing her blanket. Perhaps there were more important things to think about than her viral video.

"Each Super will be assigned to a homeroom," Waller announced. "We'll forgo math and a couple of other classes for now and in the near future, instead focusing on Weaponomics, Flyers' Ed, and phys ed. Please check the homeroom sheets in the hallway and head there immediately. Your teachers will fill you in on more."

There was a rush out the door as the students ran around her. Left alone in the empty auditorium, Supergirl whipped off her baseball cap, sunglasses, and toga to reveal her iconic costume underneath . . . the one that made Crazy Quilt cry. The one she now wore with confidence. Supergirl flashed back to her first day at Super Hero High, and to her training, her friends, and to what lay before her. Standing tall with her hands on her hips, all became clear.

More than anything in the world, Supergirl wanted to be . . . a super hero.

★

As Supergirl joined the Supers in the hall, she passed Waller, who was talking to Barbara.

"I don't mind the overtime," Babs was saying. "I look forward to it. Anything I can do to help Super Hero High."

"Great," Waller said. "I'll talk to your father about it."

Soon, Supergirl was listening with rapt attention to everything Liberty Belle was saying. "We don't know who or what it is yet. . . ."

Off to the side, she could hear Cheetah holding court and whispering. "I heard from Green Lantern, who heard from Frost, who heard from Adam Strange, who heard from Bumblebee, who overheard Ivy telling Hawkgirl and The Flash that it's the Boom Tubes again. . . ."

"I can't wait to go into battle," Supergirl heard Cyborg announce. "I've never been more ready!"

"I'm going to sharpen my swords as soon as we get out of here," Katana told Harley, who replied, "I'm going to do a special on this called *Super Hero High Super Security Task Force.* It'll be a reality show!"

As her fellow students talked excitedly about testing their powers in a real fight, Supergirl found she couldn't join in the bravado. Though she had a keen sense of right and wrong, she wasn't looking forward to heading into battle. Instead, Supergirl wanted peace and justice, and hoped that it could be achieved without fighting. She wanted to help, not harm.

After all, Supergirl knew firsthand what destruction could do.

# CHAPTER 23

For the next few days Supergirl kept mainly to herself. Katana and Bumblebee tried to include her in their conversations, and Wonder Woman insisted that they sit together in class. With all that was going on at school, everyone felt bonded together—but Supergirl just wasn't feeling it.

As she walked through the dining hall gripping her tray, Supergirl was having trouble controlling her super-hearing again. Conversations began swirling around her, mixing in with memories of conversations past.

"The tests are back. It's a *guadua longifolia*!" Poison Ivy said, knowingly.

"What test?" The Flash asked. "Guad lo foli who? What language are you speaking?"

"Testing that leaf," Hawkgirl reminded him. "From outside the Boom Tubes door."

"My numbers are through the roof," Harley boasted.

"We need to keep an eye on everyone," Waller said.

*"Guadua longifolia!"* Poison Ivy said again. "That's the scientific name for bamboo."

Supergirl looked over at Vice Principal Grodd, who was sitting at the far end of the faculty table munching on a big bowl of bamboo and wiping his sweaty brow with his red handkerchief. The Junior Detective Society members were eyeing him, too.

★

With the school on alert, their super hero training was even more important than ever. Supergirl knew that she had to regain her dignity during the upcoming speed test. She'd been training hard with Barbara, who told her, "Believe in your super self."

"I believe in my super self," Supergirl repeated as she stood at the starting line. "I believe in my super self."

Wonder Woman stood nearby for moral support. "You can do it, Supergirl!" she cheered. Katana, Hawkgirl, Poison Ivy, and Bumblebee nodded as the red light on Harley's video camera lit up so she could start filming.

Supergirl took a deep breath.

Wildcat called out, "Three . . . two . . . one . . . go!!!!"

Before anyone had a chance to blink, Supergirl took off running. Her legs were going so fast they were a blur, and her arms pumped to gain more speed. She felt good. In control. Nothing could stop her!

"Ninety-five!" Wildcat called out as Supergirl streaked past the finish line. "You got a ninety-five on the speed test!"

But Supergirl didn't have time to bask in her glory. Just then, the security alarm sounded, and without breaking stride, she instinctively headed toward the Boom Tubes door.

★

The first one there, Supergirl was soon joined by Principal Waller. Though The Wall didn't possess any of the traditional superpowers, she could seem faster, smarter, and stronger than most of her students by sheer willpower.

Brushing past Supergirl, Waller bent down. "Dents and scratches," she said, astonished. "These doors are supposed to be damage proof."

"What do you think happened?" Supergirl asked. Could someone have broken into the Boom Tubes? she wondered. Was there someone else at school as curious about the Boom Tubes as she was? Someone who was willing to risk breaching security? Or did someone have a more sinister plan in mind?

Waller shook her head. "This is a mystery."

The Junior Detective Society arrived. Without speaking, the trio set to work. The Flash dusted for prints. Bumblebee used an X-Acto ruler to measure the indents. Hawkgirl took photos.

"Give me a full report," Waller said to Grodd, who stood nearby awaiting orders. "Continue with super hero training.

We've got this under control for now. Keep Barbara Gordon in the loop. She's on her way. I've got to make sure the rest of the campus is secure!" The Wall ordered as she marched down the corridor. Vice Principal Grodd went in the other direction.

"Animalistic," The Flash noted, still staring at the scratches.

"Gorilla-istic?" Hawkgirl asked.

"Another one," Poison Ivy commented, holding up a bamboo leaf.

"Gorilla Grodd!" they said in unison.

"He *is* a reformed villain," The Flash said.

"And there was that bamboo leaf left here last time there was a security breach," Hawkgirl added.

"He gets nervous when anyone talks to him," Poison Ivy pointed out.

"Is that enough evidence to go on?" Supergirl asked.

All the Supers looked at her, surprised she was even there.

"Just asking," she said. "Never mind."

# CHAPTER 24

" . . . **SO**, in conclusion," Principal Waller told the assembly, "Super Hero High will continue to be on alert until otherwise noted. Wonder Woman will be organizing a group of volunteers to monitor the Boom Tubes door around the clock, and . . . Yes, Beast Boy?"

"If we volunteer, does this mean we can get out of class?" he asked. Several Supers crossed their fingers.

Waller sighed. "Wonder Woman is in charge of scheduling. This is nothing to joke about. The security of Super Hero High is in question! That is all—you are dismissed!"

With speed and efficiency worthy of an Amazon princess, Wonder Woman organized the volunteers. Most everyone wanted to participate. Some Supers even volunteered for multiple shifts. The teachers agreed to monitor the monitors. Granny Goodness offered to supply cookies and hot chocolate to those who took the night shift.

Excitement was in the air. Everyone had a theory. This wasn't like when the teachers' cars were found in trees, or when someone melted all the lockers. This was no joke.

ALERT!!!!

When the Save the Day Alarm rang, the students hesitated, waiting for Bumblebee, or someone—anyone—to tell them it was just a drill. Only no one did, and in the nanosecond it took for this to sink in, every student at Super Hero High was ready to go. This was what they had been training for. Suddenly, everyone was serious. Even Beast Boy.

Wonder Woman led the charge, barking out orders. There was no time for social graces. Supergirl jetted up in the air and joined Wondy as they flew to Metropolis side by side. As they rounded the roof at the corner of the Ace Athletic Supplies building, Wonder Woman pointed to something. Using her super-vision, Supergirl homed in on a ten-foot-tall woman punching a hole in the window of Eclipso Jewels. The woman grabbed a fistful of diamond necklaces and shoved them into her oversized handbag. Before anyone could intervene a security guard showed up. The woman grinned and punched him hard, sending him flying. As he fell to the ground, Miss Martian cried, "It's Giganta!" before turning invisible.

Instantly, Wonder Woman yelled, "Supers on the ground— Harley, Cheetah, Katana, Ivy, The Flash—surround the store in the Secret Snake maneuver. Supers in the air—Bumblebee,

Hawkgirl, Beast Boy, Green Lantern, and the rest of you—split into four quadrants and form the Danger Diamond formation, ready to attack. . . ."

As Wonder Woman continued calling plays like a quarterback, Supergirl waited for her instructions. It seemed like every Super from Super Hero High was given an assignment but her. Was Wondy upset that she had tried to upstage her with the strength test, using Beast Boy the way she had? Or perhaps she'd been presumptuous to fly next to Wonder Woman on this dangerous mission. With everyone getting into position, Wonder Woman looked at Supergirl and wrinkled her nose. "What are you waiting for, Supergirl? You're with me!"

Supergirl's heart soared as the duo sped toward the Eclipso storefront. "Giganta! Put the jewels down right now!" Wonder Woman called out, her voice strong.

Giganta looked up, surprised to be surrounded by an army of teen super heroes on the ground and in the air. Slowly, she grinned and began to grow bigger and bigger until she eclipsed the Eclipso building, her shadow almost making it look like day had turned to night.

"When she grows, she gets more aggressive," Supergirl shouted. All her research on heroes and villains had finally come in handy!

Giganta picked up a minivan and hurled it at Wonder Woman, who blocked it with her shield. Using the nearby parking lot as her personal arsenal, Giganta flung car after car as Wonder Woman deflected them.

People on the streets were cheering, but Supergirl knew it wasn't safe for spectators. A man fainted when an electric car barely missed him. Instantly, Hawkgirl swooped in and carried him to safety.

"Bumblebee!" Wonder Woman called out. "Get into position!"

Bumblebee nodded and shrank down to the size of an eraser. "Three, two, one . . . go!" Wonder Woman ordered. On command Bumblebee flew directly toward Giganta, then let go a stinger blast. Shock turned to pain as Giganta ripped a streetlight from the ground. She thrashed the light like a fly swatter at Bumblebee, who buzzed around her head, gleefully dodging and dancing, and singing, "Being a super hero is fun!"

"Watch out!" Supergirl yelled just as Giganta was about to crush Bumblebee.

With less than an inch to spare, Bumblebee swooped away. Wonder Woman tended to the civilians on the street, who were now panicking. It was up to Supergirl to contain Giganta.

Supergirl slowly rose and focused on the streetlight in Giganta's massive hand. She took a deep breath and stared intently at her target. Her heat vision beams shot out directly on the streetlight. . . .

Cheetah, who had been clearing the streets of abandoned cars so the emergency vehicles could enter, sneered. "You sure you got this, Supergirl? Remember what happened to your buddy Dinosaur Boy!"

Supergirl winced. That was all it took. The beam from her eyes went a few centimeters off course, and before she could correct herself and hit Giganta's streetlight, the huge woman yanked it out of the ray's mighty path. It was too late to stop the ray as it hit the window of a skyscraper behind her. From there, the heat ray ricocheted off the building and headed straight toward Bumblebee, who was hovering near Giganta, about to release a second stinger blast.

Supergirl gasped in horror as her heat ray nicked Bumblebee's leg. Bumblebee's scream echoed as she did a dizzying fall before turning big and landing hard on the pavement.

In a panic, Supergirl flew to her friend's side. Bumblebee's face was contorted in pain, and she was clinging to her leg where she'd been hit. Supergirl knelt next to her to comfort her.

"I'm okay," Bumblebee said bravely. One of her wings was bent. She couldn't hide her grimace. "It's not too bad."

Cheetah materialized with a first-aid kit and tended to her wound. "Supergirl," she said, "maybe you should leave the super hero-ing to the pros and everyone would be safer."

Supergirl was crushed. This was all her fault. She wasn't

helping the cause. She was hurting it . . . and her friends. Behind them, Giganta ramped up her rampage. Supergirl looked up to see Harley and a pack of Supers rushing to help Bumblebee. "Give her some room to breathe!" Supergirl said, flinging her arms back.

"Oof!" Wonder Woman cried. Supergirl had accidentally whacked her, sending her flying thirty feet backward and crashing into a billboard advertising Safe-T First Collision Insurance.

"See? Even Wonder Woman would be safer without you," Cheetah sniped as she tore the cloth bandage with her teeth. Katana helped Bumblebee limp to safety as Poison Ivy checked on Wonder Woman, who was only slightly dazed. Harley turned her camera back to Giganta.

Enraged, Giganta was now so big that when she grinned at the office workers on the ninth floor of the adjoining building, they all flung themselves to the floor and cowered under their desks.

"Do something, Supergirl!" someone called out. "Help us!"

Supergirl couldn't move. Her brain told her to fly, to use her powers, to do something, anything, but her body was frozen.

"Don't worry, Supergirl. I got this," Cheetah said, motioning to a group of Supers. "Follow me, everyone!" she ordered as she raced toward danger with lightning speed.

With Cheetah at the helm, the Supers proceeded to take Giganta down in spectacular fashion.

Too rattled to join in, Supergirl watched the chaos around her as if she were a mere spectator or someone tuning in to "Harley's Quinntessentials". Finally, she shook her head in defeat. "You'll be safer without me," Supergirl murmured as she flew away, leaving her fellow students to fight the battle.

# CHAPTER 25

It was no surprise that Harley's video was at the top of the TV and Internet news cycle. As Lois Lane reported in her article, "Capturing Giganta was a spectacular team effort, led in no small part by Cheetah."

The Quinntessentials exclusive had captured it all, including a "biggest hits" section featuring battle scenes, plus cutaways of Supergirl accidentally harming her friend and then fleeing the scene. Though this had happened days earlier, Supergirl was still feeling the embarrassment, especially since Cheetah and Star Sapphire were pouring on the snide remarks.

"Supergirl, forget how to fight?"

"I like your coward! Oh, I mean, *courage!*"

"If you're a team player, which team are you on? Theirs?"

Supergirl wished she didn't have to go to school. She wished she could just stay in bed and hide.

"Rise and shine, lazybones!" Bumblebee called. "We've got a test today!"

A test. That was the last thing Supergirl needed.

★

As she approached class, Supergirl saw Miss Martian. She was appearing and disappearing as she made her way down the hall.

"Hi, Supergirl," she said shyly. "I'm sorry you're so sad."

There was no hiding anything from Miss Martian.

"Yes, well. You know," Supergirl said.

Miss Martian nodded. "I do know," she replied. "And so do you."

"What do I know?" Supergirl asked. But by then, Miss Martian had disappeared again.

★

Supergirl kept wondering what Miss Martian had meant. What was she supposed to know? What was she supposed to do? As Supergirl ventured outside there were students everywhere working out in pairs, in groups, and individually. Poison Ivy was talking to a row of rosebushes, urging them to blossom and praising them when they did. Katana was tossing knives in the air, as if she were slicing at clouds, then whirling around and catching them . . . all while blindfolded.

And The Flash was speeding across campus at such a dizzying pace that it looked like he was racing himself. Supergirl loved seeing everyone's dedication. That's when she realized what Miss Martian meant.

Despite her feelings of failure, Supergirl wanted to succeed at Super Hero High. She wanted to be like her peers who were dedicating themselves to helping make the world safe. She could do it, she knew she could. But it was going to take a lot of hard work.

With renewed vigor, Supergirl headed to phys ed, pulling her shoulders back and strolling confidently into class. She mentally prepared for what lay ahead.

"Listen up, Supers," Wildcat growled. "This is the obstacle course. Not some elementary save, like rescuing pets!"

"Like Rainbow," Hawkgirl noted.

"Exactly. Good example," Wildcat barked. "That little guy just can't seem to stay out of trouble. No, this test is serious and measures your ability to save your own life and the lives of others."

Wildcat adjusted his cowl and looked around at the students. One seemed to stand taller than the rest. "Supergirl," he said. "You're up! Let's see what you're made of."

There was a low murmur as Supergirl approached the starting line. In the days that had passed, Supergirl had made it a point to avoid her friends and fellow students whenever possible, not speaking to anyone. It didn't mean, however, that no one spoke about her.

"She thinks she's all that," Frost said as she applied her ice-white lipstick in the girls' restroom.

"She's none of that," Cheetah said as she strolled down the hallway. "I was the one who saved the day."

"Why is she even here?" Star Sapphire asked after Weaponomics. "I thought this was a school for super heroes, not super goofs."

"Three . . . two . . . one . . . go!" Wildcat shouted. "Supergirl! I said, GO. Do something, don't just stand there. The clock is ticking!"

"Huh? Oh, sorry," she said, trying to shake off the comments she'd heard the past couple of days.

As Supergirl bounced off the electrified pillars and lumbered through the laser forest, she didn't feel a thing. Even being showered with lead cannons didn't faze her, and by the time she struggled to the end of the obstacle course, Supergirl had broken a school record . . . for the all-time lowest score.

*So much for showing everyone what I'm made of,* she thought.

★

Later that night, Supergirl went to the library to work on a report. She would have gone earlier, but she couldn't face seeing anyone else. Hawkgirl was sitting alone at one of the heavy wooden desks surrounded by piles of books and newspapers so old they weren't online.

From behind a nearby bookcase, Supergirl watched Granny totter up to Hawkgirl. *"The Super-Villain Compendium,"* the librarian said, blowing the dust off the book's leather cover. "I've marked some interesting sections for you, Hawkgirl. It's admirable that you're going back into history to try to find out what's happening now and who we should be wary of."

As Granny shuffled off, leaning heavily on her cane, Supergirl used her super-vision to see Hawkgirl open to the page Granny had bookmarked. There was a photo of Gorilla Grodd in attack mode as terrified citizens raced away from him. Supergirl gasped, then covered her mouth, but it was too late. Hawkgirl looked up to see Supergirl step out of the shadows.

"'Gorilla Grodd commands gorilla army in attempt to conquer Central City,'" Hawkgirl read out loud.

Both Supers looked grim.

★

Supergirl sat on the old bell tower ledge, staring into the night sky. She liked it here. Sure, the Amethyst Tower was triumphant, shiny, and new. But this place seemed more like home. Smaller. Safer. Unassuming.

There had been a couple more Alerts lately. The Boom

Tubes again. Could it be Grodd who was trying to get to them? Supergirl thought about the awkward vice principal with his ill-fitting jacket, his penchant for bananas and bamboo, and even his clumsy caveman-like banter. He didn't seem to fit in at the school, but then, Supergirl ruminated, neither did she.

Suddenly, there was creaking on the wooden stairs that led to the top of the tower. Supergirl whipped around, ready for trouble.

"Hey, Supergirl!"

Supergirl relaxed. It was Barbara Gordon. Oh, how she'd missed her. But with all that had been happening, Supergirl had avoided everyone, even Babs.

Barbara pushed aside the old rope bell cord, accidentally disturbing a flock of bats perched above. As the squeaking creatures rushed through the tower, Supergirl closed her eyes and covered her head against the onslaught of small black-winged creatures. When she opened her eyes, Babs was smiling contently as the wind from their fluttering wings blew her hair. Both girls watched the bats flitter past the full moon.

"Everybody thinks bats are creepy, but not me," Barbara said, adjusting her glasses. She didn't seem surprised to find Supergirl up in the tower. But then, not much fazed her. "They make the best of what they have. They don't have night vision, but they use the talents they have."

The two sat in silence. Supergirl liked that it didn't feel

awkward. It felt comfortable. "Hey, Barbara," she finally said.

"Hmmm?" Babs answered, watching a couple of displaced bats seamlessly join the rest flying in formation.

"Do you think it could be Grodd who's trying to access the Boom Tubes?" Supergirl ventured. "There was this leaf that Ivy identified as bamboo, and we've found it not once, but twice, after someone tried to break in the doors. And then Hawkgirl uncovered evidence that Grodd used to be a villain and even had his own army—he attacked and tried to take over Central City!"

When Supergirl was done with her theories, Barbara was quiet. Supergirl thought that perhaps her friend was processing everything she had heard and would come up with a plan to capture Gorilla Grodd. Barbara was good at that. She was what Mr. Fox in Weaponomics would call "strategic," only instead of lasers or lassos, Barbara Gordon's secret weapon was her smarts.

"I'm not sure it's such a great idea to judge Vice Principal Grodd based on his past actions and/or accusations and very loose circumstantial evidence. Supposedly, he's been reformed. If there's one thing I learned from my father, Police Commissioner Gordon," Babs said in measured tones, "it's that we must give every person a chance. Don't take anything at face value. Gather your facts. Make an informed decision. Gut-check it. Then proceed."

"Gut-check?" Supergirl asked.

Barbara nodded. "How does it feel? What does your heart

say? Facts and figures are great, but they're not everything."

Barbara fell silent then. Supergirl wondered if she was mad at her for jumping to conclusions about Grodd.

"Supergirl, it's been so nice knowing you," Babs said, sounding glum.

*She* is *mad at me!* Supergirl thought. Or wait. Maybe it was something even worse. *Am I getting kicked out of Super Hero High?* she wondered. That was it, wasn't it? Barbara had found out before she did!

"My contract is almost up," Barbara continued. "I won't be working here much longer."

This was even worse news than she had guessed. This wasn't about her. It was about Babs. "But you love working here!" Supergirl cried.

"Tell me about it," Barbara said, fiddling with her Utility Belt. "But I was only on a short-term contract, and my dad's not too keen on me keeping this job. He wants me to focus on my schoolwork now. He's got this crazy idea that I'm going to graduate and get a scholarship to a great business school and become an accountant or something safe like that."

"No, no, no," Supergirl protested. "We need you here. Super Hero High needs you."

"That's not what he says," Babs said, trying to force a smile and failing.

Supergirl was silent, drinking in the information. "But you are so totally awesome in every way. I wish I could be like you," she finally said. Supergirl wrapped her cape around herself for comfort.

"An awesome, fearless, fun tech engineer with zero superpowers?" Barbara joked.

"You have powers!" Supergirl insisted, jumping up. "If only I had one-tenth the smarts you do. Your brain is your superpower, Babs. You know high-tech better than anyone. Plus, you never hurt anyone, unlike . . . well, me." Supergirl waved her hand at the world below her. "If I were a non-Super, the Earth would be safer," she said softly.

Now it was Barbara's turn to stand up. She looked serious. "I want you to stop feeling sorry for yourself," she said matter-of-factly. "It's because of you that one day the world will be safer. You're here at Super Hero High to learn how to be a super hero. And unlike so many of the others, you just got your powers a few months ago. Do your best, Supergirl. That's all anyone is asking of you."

Supergirl gasped. The words were so familiar. She flashed back to her mother saying, "Always do your best, Kara, and you'll be fine." When she tuned back in, Barbara was running down a list of Supergirl's powers, ending with, "And you can fly! I'd give anything to fly—like a bat—just once."

"You and your bats," Supergirl said with affection. "I should call you Batgirl."

"I like that. Batgirl," she said, trying the name out with a dramatic sweep of her arm. *"Batgirl."*

Supergirl held out her hand. "Join me, Batgirl."

Barbara looked quizzically at her friend, but took her hand without question.

"Hang on," Supergirl shouted as she soared into the sky. "We're going for a ride!"

As the two friends flew over Super Hero High, then around Metropolis and beyond, they could not stop grinning. The moon cast its glow as the stars winked a path for them. Neither spoke the entire time. They didn't need to. This was a flight they'd remember for the rest of their lives.

# CHAPTER 26

During breakfast a few days later, Supergirl was being extremely careful not to tilt her tray as she headed to the table, when Barbara barged into the dining hall. "Supergirl," she said, out of breath. Startled, Supergirl watched as her sunny-side up eggs slid off the plate and splattered on the floor.

"Where's the Junior Detective Society?" Barbara said in a rush.

"Uh, here?" The Flash said, from the table behind them.

"Join us," Bumblebee said, scooting closer to Hawkgirl.

Janitor Parasite muttered as he cleaned up the mess.

"Sorry," Supergirl began, but his glare cut her off.

"My interstellar transmission tracking device went into overdrive," Barbara informed them. "I've intercepted an off-Earth message that seems to be tied to the Boom Tubes!"

"What is it?" Hawkgirl asked.

"Tell us!" The Flash insisted.

"Yes, yes, I can't wait," Poison Ivy blurted out.

Barbara took a gulp of Hawkgirl's water, then said, "The message is . . . 'Soon our army will rise!'"

The silence was loud.

Supergirl was stunned.

It was The Flash who finally spoke. "We've got to tell Waller immediately!"

"She's at the semiannual How to Deal with Teens and Their Angst, Anger, and Agony Conference," Barbara said.

"This is critical information. The safety of the world could depend on it," Bumblebee interjected.

Supergirl cleared her throat. The Junior Detective Society looked surprised to see her. "I'll fly there and tell her," she offered. "That way you guys can start working with this new information."

★

Less than an hour later, at an emergency assembly, the principal stood onstage as the teachers and Vice Principal Grodd sat behind her in solidarity.

"Our information tells us that there is danger lurking and that Super Hero High may be the initial primary target. If these villains aren't stopped, the entire world and beyond will be in jeopardy." Waller looked more serious than usual, which was quite a feat. No one in the audience moved. "We don't know where the infiltration will come from, but we do know that the Boom Tubes are most likely an interception point. We must be vigilant and on guard at all times. For now, regular classes are suspended, and will be replaced by extended Weaponomics and battle training. Everyone, be alert!"

There was a low murmur among the students. Some were scared, some were worried, and others were eager to finally test their battle skills outside of the classroom. They all knew this was serious. As if Waller could read the room, she added, "This is not a game. Lives are at stake. We must work together to fight this. Do you hear me?"

"Yes, Principal Waller!" the Supers yelled.

"What?" Waller asked, cupping her ear.

"YES, PRINCIPAL WALLER!" they yelled again, this time rising up from their seats.

★

It just didn't seem right. There was something going on with the Boom Tubes security door, but no one could figure out what. A general feeling of unrest floated among the students and the faculty.

"It looks even more battered," Supergirl said, bending down to examine the fresh dents in the door. "Look!"

Hawkgirl nodded. "It's like someone or something is trying to get in."

"Double duty!" Waller proclaimed as she did the first of

many night rounds, checking to make sure the school was secured. "Triple duty, if necessary!"

Supergirl looked over at Katana, who nodded and motioned to her sword as if saying, "I dare them."

"Katana and I will take the night shift," Supergirl volunteered.

As the girls settled into their sleeping bags, someone said, "Hot cocoa with marshmallows?" Both turned to see Granny balancing a tray heavy with cookies and steaming hot mugs. "Drink up, dearies," she said. "There's plenty more where that came from."

Supergirl drained her mug, then asked for more. The warm, chocolatey goodness filled her belly and gave her a pleasant feeling of satisfaction.

"Katana," she said, nudging her friend. "Wake up! We're supposed to be guarding the Boom Tubes."

Katana sat up and rubbed her eyes. It was after midnight. "I must have dozed off." She took another sip of her hot chocolate, then reached for a cookie. Some sparkly sugar sprinkles fell onto her costume.

"We've got to stay awake," Supergirl insisted. Her eyelids felt heavy.

"Awake!" Katana repeated, trying to blink away sleep.

★

"This is how you guard the Boom Tubes door?" Hawkgirl said, looking stern. "You are not following protocol!"

Supergirl and Katana bolted upright. They had fallen asleep on the floor. There were new scratches on the bottom of the door.

Hawkgirl shook her head and Poison Ivy looked embarrassed for them. "You two, go on and get breakfast," Hawkgirl said with her hands on her hips. "We'll take over now."

As Supergirl sat down for breakfast, she looked over at Wonder Woman, who had scribbled all over several sheets of paper. She was absentmindedly shoveling cereal into her mouth. Wayward pieces of colorful sugary bits were scattered around. "I'm mapping out a plan," she explained, turning a piece of paper upside down. "Only, I'm having trouble keeping the coordinates straight."

Supergirl looked at the papers but couldn't make out what they meant. At the next table she could hear The Flash and Bumblebee talking. "Look at him," The Flash said.

"He doesn't even care, does he?" Bumblebee said, pouring more honey into her tea. "I mean, to be so blatant? Really?"

Supergirl followed their gaze. It ended at Gorilla Grodd, who was enjoying a huge bowl of bamboo. She tried to remember what Barbara had said about jumping to conclusions. Still, there *was* that article Granny had unearthed about Grodd's criminal past and the bamboo leaf found by the Boom Tubes doors. Twice. Coincidence?

During her Battle Refresher drill, Supergirl did her best to focus on what the teachers were saying. She asked questions and made sure to help in every way she could. Plus, she was super-friendly and encouraging with everyone. She had to be. Supergirl was determined to put the disaster with Giganta behind her. Bumblebee had seemed to forgive her. And so had many of the others.

Everyone was hyper focused on strength, powers, and weapons training. Some were perhaps too focused. With adrenaline surging, accidents were happening at a much higher rate than usual. In a strange way, Supergirl was glad she wasn't the only one messing up. At the same time, she chided herself for even thinking this. Lives were at stake, as Waller had impressed upon them. Everyone needed to be at their best.

Not wanting to panic anyone, The Wall instructed the teens to make their days as normal as possible. That meant regular meals, regular bedtimes—except for the volunteers on guard duty.

★

"Look at this," Harley was saying. They were in the computer lab. Supergirl peered over her shoulder. On the screen was a

Web broadcast by Lois Lane. She was doing an analysis of who could be amassing an army.

"I guess everyone knows," Supergirl said.

"It's hard to keep a secret around here," Harley answered, smiling sweetly, then letting go of a big laugh and doing a backflip. "I love a good secret, and so does this!" she said, holding up her camera.

"But it's not just at Super Hero High that super heroes are being on guard," Lois reported. "My sources tell me there's unrest on another quadrant of outer space at this very moment. That means it could be Darkseid or Mongul or Massacre or any number of evil villains who are itching to take over Earth."

Hawkgirl stepped into the room. "You have a phone call," she said to Supergirl. "It's your aunt Martha. She sounds worried."

Supergirl took the phone. "Yes, no, yes, I'm safe. Well, I mean, I'm here to keep you and everyone else safe. Yes, Aunt Martha, I'll be careful. I promise. Give my best to Uncle Jonathan. What? Oh, okay. Hello, Uncle Jonathan, yes, I can tell she's worried. I know. I know. Okay, I'll call you later."

Hawkgirl nodded in sympathy. "Abuela Muñoz is worried out of her mind," she said. "I'm not sure what's worse—having Supers in the family who know firsthand the kind of danger we could be put in, or having non-Supers who believe everything they see on TV."

Supergirl gave her an understanding smile and shrugged.

"Is it true?" Barbara asked, rushing in. "I just saw Lois Lane's report. Not only are we possibly under siege, but there are even more battles brewing elsewhere. What can I do to help?"

Supergirl looked at her friend. Barbara wanted to help so badly. Then it hit her! "I think I know," she said. "Come with me, Babs."

Supergirl dragged her over to Wonder Woman, who by now was practically buried under a mound of papers. "How's it going?" Supergirl asked.

"It's *not* going," Wonder Woman said, sounding uncharacteristically dejected. "I thought I had a great plan, but it's so hard to map it out."

"I know how you can get this done," Supergirl said confidently. "Barbara here can help."

"Welcome to the team," Wonder Woman said to Barbara while shaking her hand.

"Ow." Barbara flexed her fingers to make sure they were still working. "I'm not sure how my dad would feel about me being on the team. He's always telling me not to do anything dangerous. This week he suggested I be a florist."

"Ivy accidentally exploded the science lab again last week doing an experiment on killer thorns," Supergirl pointed out. "That wasn't safe. Besides, this isn't official. We just want to borrow your brains to help sort all this out."

Wonder Woman pointed to the mess of papers scattered everywhere. Barbara picked up a couple and studied them. "Hmmm . . . okay. Right. I see what you're trying to do." She pulled out her B.A.T. computer and began punching in numbers.

Supergirl looked over her shoulder. "Wow, your computer does everything!"

Barbara laughed. "I wish! It's hyped up since I added mega memory, fluid dynamic calculation abilities, hologram graphics, and other stuff, but it's not like it's a Mother Box."

"A what?" Wonder Woman asked.

"A Mother Box," Barbara said, scanning in more data. "That's a small supercomputer created on Apokolips. It's said they can do almost anything from coordinating Boom Tubes teleportation to energy manipulation." Barbara's eyes sparkled with mischief. "I'm going to ask Santa for one!"

"What's happening?" Supergirl exclaimed as a long set of numbers, letters, and symbols scrolled in a circular pattern on the computer screen.

"What are we looking at?" Wonder Woman said, confused. "I'm getting dizzy."

"One moment . . . ," Barbara said, typing quickly. "I ran some numbers using your coordinates, sketches, and notes. Then I applied my alpha beta delta triplicate trig formula, and voilà!"

Supergirl and Wonder Woman blinked. Nothing was registering. Babs started laughing at herself. "I get so into this stuff I forget that most people think I'm speaking gibberish. Here, look." She turned her screen toward them. "I've mapped out and dissected what you were trying to figure out on your papers." Wonder Woman's eyes widened. "It's your plan!" Barbara said. "I've just streamlined it and corrected some of the coordinates."

Supergirl beamed. "See, Super Hero High needs you!

Besides, it's more dangerous not to get involved than it is to help."

"I feel funny working alongside all of you," Babs confided as she sent Wonder Woman's plans to the printer.

"Why?" Supergirl asked. "You've been working here as long as I've known you."

"True," Barbara said, nodding. "But that was in a support capacity. Fixing your computers, setting up security for Waller, that sort of thing. But now you've asked me to help come up with strategies and fight alongside you—figuratively, of course. That's something completely different. I mean, you guys are trained to be super heroes—"

"We're not fully trained *yet*," Supergirl corrected her. "Remember, just a few months ago I didn't even have any powers."

"Well, that may be," Barbara said, "but look at you now. Plus, you look the part of a super hero. I look the part of a nerd."

Supergirl appraised Babs's black crop top, jeans, and lace-up boots. She thought she looked just fine. But suddenly, Supergirl had an idea so awesome that she startled herself!

★

"Black," Katana said, drawing furiously. "Black, sleek, simple . . ."

Supergirl leaned over and took a peek at Katana's

sketchpad. "Perfect!" she said as Katana triumphantly slammed her pencil down.

"Let's raid Crazy Quilt's fabric closet," Katana said, already out the door. "I can quickly stitch it together."

"I don't know if we should," Supergirl said, hesitating.

Katana chuckled. "Rule follower! You sound like Hawkgirl. Of course we should," she insisted. "This is for the good of Super Hero High, the good of the world, and the good of the universe!"

"Okay!" Supergirl brightened up. "When you put it that way, we sort of have to."

As the girls made their way quietly down the corridors toward Crazy Quilt's classroom, Supergirl thought she saw a small monster scamper around a corner. *Bigfoot again? Nah. Grodd?*

"Um, did you see that?" she asked.

"See what?" Katana said as she silently opened one of the classroom doors.

"Never mind," Supergirl said, figuring she was seeing things again.

★

"This is for you," Supergirl said, practically bubbling with barely contained excitement. She held out a plain white box. "Katana made it."

"Open it! Open it!" Wonder Woman said to Barbara.

"What could it be? Or is it just the box, because that would be nice, too. A box to put things in!"

"I hope you like it," Katana said. Though she was normally fierce, with an I-can-do-anything attitude, she looked just a little nervous.

Babs lifted the lid off the box. "Pow! For me?" she cried, holding up the simple black unitard.

"There's a belt for all your tools and matching gloves, too," Katana said, enormously cheered by Barbara's huge grin.

"Thank you!" Barbara said, hugging them both. "I love it! Oh, but let's not tell my dad, okay? For now, anyway. He'll get all weird if he knows I have a super hero costume. You know how he feels about me doing anything dangerous."

Before Barbara could try on her new outfit, the security alarm began to blare. Waller's voice blasted over the PA system. "ALERT! Activity alert at the Boom Tubes!"

# CHAPTER 28

Several Supers and teachers stood staring, not sure what they were looking for. "Stand back!" Waller ordered. "We don't know what's happening yet. Our isolation motion sensors detected movement at the door that did not match the DNA of anyone from Super Hero High."

The blinking warning lights cast a red glow over the area.

Disobeying the principal's orders, Barbara pushed her way to the front. Waller was about to chide her, but stepped aside. Using her equipment, Babs began to analyze the door. When she knelt down and shined a blue light on the door, deep grooves became clear.

"I need an electro marginalizing magnetic sieve and a metal conductor to play it off of," she said.

No one moved.

"Talk in terms we can understand," Supergirl suggested kindly.

"Right. Okay. Metal and a conductor, stat!" Barbara said,

palms up like a surgeon awaiting her operating tools.

In a flash, Wonder Woman handed over her cuffs and Katana gave up one of her swords. Cyborg offered himself up as the metal conductor. Barbara tinkered with the weapons, attaching them to wires and doodads, then plugged the whole thing into the back of Cyborg's head.

"You're the best metal conductor I've ever seen," Babs told him. He blushed, then, remembering the seriousness of the situation, stood still as Barbara waved the device centimeters away from the door. The arrows on the small monitor on the box began to go haywire.

"What?" Waller asked.

Barbara looked grim. "Clearly this isn't the first time there's been a breach attempt. From the angle and depth and length of these marks, my analysis shows that the seemingly impenetrable metal has been put under intense pressure. Look, the metal fatigue factor is out of control!" When she held up her monitor everyone nodded, even though they didn't know what they were looking at. "I know!" Barbara cried, adding, "I'm afraid that someone or some*thing* is very determined to take this door down."

★

Though they tried not to show it, many of the students were nervous. It was one thing to learn about villains and criminals, but this would be the first time many Super Hero

High students would face one in person. Who was this thing that was so determined to get into the Boom Tubes, and why? Miss Martian was nowhere to be seen, though she was always around. Beast Boy didn't tell nearly as many jokes. Even Cheetah's snipes had noticeably less bite.

Only Wonder Woman seemed to be herself. Confident and courageous, and going about her business with a level head, she conferred with Barbara, smiling and waving at everyone.

Nights were always the hardest time for Supergirl, and now with the threat of evil so close, she couldn't sleep at all. What if instead of helping the cause, she messed up and jeopardized it? It had happened before.

She tossed and turned, and turned and tossed, and finally her body was so exhausted that it gave in to a fitful sleep, which led to a disturbing dream, or a painful memory . . .

"Go, Kara! Hurry!" her mom said with urgency.

Kara steadied herself on the handrail of the stairs, climbing up until she stood in the cockpit entry of the spaceship.

"Mom! Dad! C'mon!" she cried, waving them in.

Alura climbed the steps to meet her daughter, holding out a crystal necklace. She clasped it firmly around Kara's neck. "This way I'll always be with you."

"What do you mean?" Kara asked, holding the crystal in her hand.

Her mother pushed a button. It closed the door

between them. Kara began banging on the porthole window in the door from the inside. "No! Mom! Dad! You have to come with me! PLEASE!"

★

Supergirl awoke gasping for air. It felt like someone had poured a whole bucket of water on her face. She sat up with a start and was surprised to find Barbara, Harley, and Hawkgirl surrounding her bed.

"Are you okay?" Barbara asked. Her brow was furrowed in worry.

"Here, drink this," Bumblebee said. She handed Supergirl a mug of warm lemon honey tea.

"You were crying," Hawkgirl said.

Supergirl was still holding on to her necklace. When she let go it stopped glowing.

"Come on," Wonder Woman called from the hallway. "It's going to be a big day. Maybe we'll come face to face with the Boom Tubes perpetrator! Everyone, please make sure you eat a good breakfast. You're going to need all the energy you can get."

Supergirl gripped her mug of tea, still reeling from her memories of Krypton. And now this. She wondered if facing the unknown was something she was just going to have to get used to.

# PART
# THREE

# CHAPTER 29

Instead of following her friends to the dining hall, Supergirl did what she always did when she wanted to clear her head. She went to the library.

"It seemed so real," she said to Granny Goodness, recounting her dream. "And the pain was incredible. I can still feel it."

"Dear, dear orphan child," Granny said. "As long as I'm here, you have family. You know that, don't you?"

When Granny asked again, Supergirl nodded, not wanting to hurt her feelings.

"That's my girl!" Granny said, smiling brightly.

Supergirl's mind had already wandered away. She didn't notice when Granny touched her necklace and for a brief moment it turned black.

Granny pulled her hand back, still smiling.

★

Supergirl stood at the starting line of the empty Flyers' Ed track. There was little time left to get her powers under control. She felt uncertain. The clock was ticking. Supergirl looked at Barbara. She couldn't tell what her friend was thinking, only that she looked serious.

"Are you ready?" Barbara asked, raising her stopwatch in the air. Supergirl nodded, her eyes staring straight ahead. "Okay," Barbara said. "Three . . . two . . . one . . . GO!"

Supergirl burst into the air and headed straight toward a series of staggered poles.

"Obstacle one," Barbara called out, amplifying her voice via her wrist computer. "Tap each pole."

Supergirl proceeded to hit the first pole, breaking it in two. She watched in horror as the top half ricocheted around the course.

"Sorry!" Supergirl called out. Her nerves had gotten the better of her. "I am so sorry!" She was glad it was just Barbara here and not any of her fellow Supers.

Barbara shook her head. "Time to stop apologizing, Supergirl," she ordered. "You're here to learn—and that sometimes means making mistakes. Don't be sorry for learning!"

Supergirl nodded again, took a deep breath, and focused on continuing on her flight path. "Obstacle two: Lasers," she heard Barbara call out. Mustering her confidence, she flew between the lasers zapping out at her from all angles. Just then, one laser nicked her sneaker, causing her to whip around. Supergirl's eyes flashed red, striking the laser blaster and causing a massive explosion.

Without missing a beat, Barbara opened an umbrella as debris rained down. She'd anticipated this.

"Oops! Sor— I mean, good learning experience!" Supergirl said, continuing down the course.

"Obstacle three: Tunnel of Doom!" Barbara shouted. "Go!"

Supergirl zoomed as fast as she could inside the tunnel as it shook and rattled from within. Covered in green sticky goop, she soared out the other end and zipped toward the final obstacle course. She smacked the finish button and was surprised when it crumbled. Her heart sank when she looked at the electronic scoreboard: 13 out of 100.

"Supergirl," Barbara said sternly. "Better to get things right than to get them fast."

"I'm a failure!" Supergirl wailed.

"No you're not," Barbara reassured her. "You're learning. No one expected you to be an instant incredible super hero. Why do you think you're at Super Hero High? Why do you think anyone is here? Training, learning to use their powers and skills." Barbara's voice began to rise. "Supergirl, if I had half a chance of going to a school as amazing as this, I'd . . . I'd . . ."

"You'd what?" Supergirl asked.

Babs looked embarrassed and then shook it off. "You've been given a great opportunity," she said, changing the subject. "It's up to you what you do with it. But can I tell you something, as your friend?"

Supergirl nodded hesitantly. She wasn't sure she wanted to hear what Barbara was going to say. Was she going to tell her she was a failure? Was she going to lecture her? Would she tell her to give it up, or worse—was Barbara going to give up on her?

Babs took a deep breath and looked straight at Supergirl. "Self-pity doesn't look good on you," she said. "Supergirl, you *must* believe in your super self."

"I don't know . . . ," Supergirl began.

"How *will* you ever know if you don't try?" Barbara challenged her, sounding frustrated. "You can do this! Listen, if you don't believe in your super self, how can anyone else believe in you?"

Supergirl had never seen her friend look so serious. She was relieved that Barbara still believed in her. She clutched her crystal and closed her eyes. Then she said softly, "Believe in my super self. Believe in my super self . . ." Over and over, Supergirl repeated this mantra, her voice getting stronger each time. Finally, her eyes flew open. Everything looked clear to her.

"Bring it on!" Supergirl told Barbara. "I believe in my super self!"

And she did. Almost.

★

For the rest of the day, Supergirl felt powerful and energized. She greeted everyone in the hallways, told jokes during meals, and asked too many questions in class. It was clear to everyone that this was Supergirl 2.0. However, it was as if her recharged battery ran down at night. That was when her doubts began to creep back.

As she buried herself under her covers, Supergirl thought about how she'd injured her friend Bumblebee. It was just a nick on her leg, but it could have been so much worse. She thought about the conversations she'd overheard and her fellow students talking about her. Then there were her low scores in class and even worse, on her strength and speed tests.

The night's darkness engulfed her, and the familiar heartache began to take over. Supergirl tried to ward it off by thinking of Barbara's face when she got her costume, or the Thanksgiving feast at the Kents', or the cookies Granny baked for her. But these could not mask the memories of her parents and how much she wished she'd never needed to come here.

Supergirl hugged her pillow. What did she want? she wondered. Maybe to just start over in a place where no one knew who she was . . . or used to be.

# CHAPTER 30

"Explain to me, again, Babs . . . What does it mean when you say your contract is up?"

"It's as I told you before," Barbara explained, trying to sound nonchalant. Still, her eyes looked sad. "My dad doesn't want me working here, especially with all that's going on. He says there's one Gordon already fighting crime, and the world doesn't need another one."

"But, well, you're . . . you're . . ." Supergirl hesitated, not knowing whether she should say it out loud.

Barbara looked at her, waiting.

Finally, Supergirl blurted it out. "You're my best friend and I need you!" she exclaimed, then quickly added, "It's okay if I'm not your best friend. I mean, you must have lots of other friends at Gotham High. And since you've lived here all your life, you probably have tons of friends, but I really don't know that many people very well and . . . and . . ." She began to tear up.

Barbara laughed, making Supergirl feel small. She began to turn away in embarrassment, when Babs grabbed her shoulder. "Hey," she said, reassuringly. "Supergirl, you're my best friend, too."

Supergirl's huge smile shined on Barbara Gordon, her best friend. Then she remembered that Barbara was leaving.

"I'm going to be so sad when you're not here," Supergirl said.

"We can still visit each other," Barbara reassured her. "We can meet at Capes and Cowls and watch Steve and Wonder Woman act awkward around each other." Both girls cracked up. Then Babs got serious. "Supergirl, I have something for you." She pulled out a small package wrapped in yellow paper with a copper wire bow around it.

Supergirl smiled when she opened it.

"It's a friendship bracelet," Barbara explained as Supergirl slipped it on her wrist and fastened it tight. "I have one, too. See? But it's more than that. It's also a two-way voice transmitter, a communications device—you know, a com bracelet. That way, no matter where we are, we can always talk to each other!"

"Does it work between planets?" Supergirl asked, examining the slim metal bangle that fit perfectly around her wrist.

"Why?" Barbara joked. "You planning on taking a trip?"

Supergirl blushed and shook her head. What Babs couldn't know was that she had been thinking more and more about transferring to Korugar Academy. Now, with Barbara no longer going to be at Super Hero High, it seemed like an even better idea.

★

The more nervous Supergirl became, the less control she had over her powers. As she strolled past the admin office, she could hear a commotion inside. It got louder and louder until Supergirl realized her super-hearing was kicking in. She blinked and suddenly her X-ray vision practically put her in the principal's office.

There, Bumblebee was insisting, "That's why we suspect Vice Principal Grodd has been trying to get into the Boom Tubes and bring his gorilla army to Metropolis!" The Flash and Hawkgirl stood beside her nodding.

On Waller's desk was an evidence bag with a bamboo leaf, a copy of a damning article about Vice Principal Grodd, and a photo of the battered Boom Tubes door. Plus there was something else . . . a red handkerchief.

"Why did you wait until now to show this to me?" Waller demanded.

"We weren't one hundred percent sure," The Flash began.

"We wanted to get even more proof, but we ran out of time," Hawkgirl added. "But when we saw the handkerchief next to the door, well, it's pretty obvious who it belongs to."

"I know it's him," said Bumblebee. "I just know it!"

The Wall looked grim. She picked up the phone and began to talk. Before she hung up, someone blasted past Supergirl.

"Out of my way!" Supergirl jumped back as Vice Principal Grodd stormed into Waller's office. He smashed his massive fists on her desk, breaking it in half. "After all I've done, you're accusing me of this!" Gorilla Grodd yelled. His face was contorted in anger.

The Wall remained calm. "Grodd, I can't afford to take any chances. You're innocent until proven guilty. However, while I'm reviewing the case, I have to revoke your security clearance. I'm sorry it's come to this."

"Well, I'm sorry it's come to this . . . I quit!" Grodd bellowed, throwing his Super Hero High faculty ID on her desk. He smashed down the door as he exited, causing Supergirl to jump again. Grodd stopped and stared at her, his angry eyes fixed on her face. "What?" he asked. "Do you think I'm guilty, too?"

Supergirl was speechless. Grodd didn't wait around for her to regain her voice. As he continued through the hallway, Supergirl felt all weirded out. Like something was just not right. Maybe it was her.

Later, when Supergirl went to the dorm, Harley had just finished interviewing Wonder Woman and uploading a "Super spectacular exclusive inside report" to her channel. "Brace yourself," she told Supergirl. "I predict that the team of Wonder Woman and Supergirl can save the world!"

Wonder Woman smiled at Supergirl. "We can do it, right? Teamwork!"

Supergirl nodded without conviction. What if instead of helping Wonder Woman, she held her back? What if instead of helping to save the world, she put it in jeopardy?

★

Deep into the night Supergirl rounded the corner near the Boom Tubes door. She was surprised to find Cyborg snoring heavily and Catwoman muttering something in her sleep about "hiding the goods." Half-eaten plates of cookies and empty mugs of hot chocolate lay scattered around them. Supergirl tiptoed past.

Once at the library, she set her books on the counter. Even though the library was closed, Granny was still working. Supergirl admired her work ethic. Her parents had been hard workers, too. She noticed a small pile of bamboo leaves in Granny's open desk drawer.

Granny saw her staring and quickly shut the drawer. "I'm finding these everywhere!" she exclaimed. She acted like it wasn't uncommon for a super hero teen to be standing in front of her after midnight, holding books in one hand and a suitcase in the other.

"I'm finished with Super Hero High," Supergirl told Granny as she returned her books, confiding, "I'm going to

Korugar Academy. I'll be on the next spaceship off Earth, and there's nothing you can do to stop me!"

Supergirl waited for Granny to talk her out of it. Supergirl *wanted* Granny to talk her out of it.

The old lady checked the library books back in and nodded. "That's nice, dear," she said. Supergirl wasn't sure if the old lady had heard her, when Granny suggested, "Why wait? Just take the Boom Tubes now!"

Supergirl gasped. "No one can use them," she reminded the old woman. "They're off-limits."

"Not for you," Granny said, smiling sweetly. "You can bend unbendable steel with your bare hands. I know, I've seen you! With your strength, you could open the door and head to Korugar Academy, or wherever you want to go. No sense waiting for public transportation with the Boom Tubes at your service." She winked.

A low, menacing growl caused Supergirl to jump back. "What was that?" she asked. The growling got louder.

Granny gave off a reassuring laugh. "Oh, dearie," she said. "No need to be scared, it's just Perry."

"Who?"

Granny patted her hand. "Some grannies have poodles or parakeets. I have a pet parademon. You two should meet!"

Supergirl watched with surprise as a muscled green monster with fangs appeared from behind a bookshelf. The size of a large dog, it had pointed ears, sharp claws on its four paws, and enormous eyes that glimmered with mischief and mayhem. Something about it was too familiar for comfort.

As Granny scratched behind the monster's ears, it closed its eyes and leaned into her. His tongue drooped like a mutt's and he began to thump his leg.

"Aw, isn't he cute?" Granny said. "Perry is just the sweetest pet." She looked alarmed and then begged Supergirl, "Now, I won't tell anyone about you breaking into the Boom Tubes if you don't tell anyone about me breaking the no pets rule."

"But I'm not breaking into the Boom Tubes," Supergirl insisted. "They're dangerous!"

Granny shook her head. "Nonsense. Everyone is just overreacting. I've seen this before. It's just another one of Waller's little tests for you youngsters."

Supergirl thought about this. With all the tests that were thrown at them, it was possible.

"You want to get to Korugar Academy ASAP, and the Boom Tubes are sooner than ASAP," Granny said. "Come on, follow me! Oh, and here." She handed over a bag of cookies.

Supergirl managed a weak, confused smile as she took the bag. Granny's cookies always made everything better. Everyone said so. As they stepped over the sleeping students, Granny said softly, "Don't wake the little darlings and disturb their sweet dreams."

# CHAPTER 31

**C**yborg and Catwoman were still sound asleep.

"You open the door, get in, jump the tube to Korugar, and I'll lock it back up before anyone notices. Nothing bad can happen," Granny assured her. Perry stood by Granny's side, drooling. "You deserve to be happy, Supergirl. It's clear that even though this is a great school, Super Hero High isn't for you."

Supergirl nodded. It was as if Granny knew she had been having second thoughts about SHH. And third thoughts. And fourth thoughts . . .

"All those horrible tests," she could hear Granny saying. "The intense pressure and expectations they put on the students here are so high!

"You go, Supergirl," Granny urged as Perry panted loudly, his tongue practically sweeping the floor. "No one can force you to be here. This isn't the right place for someone as kind and sensitive as you."

Supergirl thought about how the Kents were eager for her to leave the farm, and how she failed her strength test so publicly, and about all her clumsy moves, and putting her fellow students in danger, and injuring her friends, and . . .

"Go . . . go . . . ," Granny whispered, giving her a nudge and placing a cookie in her hand. "You go, dear. They don't appreciate someone like you here."

"But we're supposed to be guarding the door, not opening it," Supergirl reminded her.

"Tsk, tsk," Granny said, shaking her head. "Waller is testing all of you, you should know that. Do you really think that if there was real danger, she'd think you kids were ready to handle it?"

*Maybe not,* Supergirl thought.

"Come, dear." Granny motioned to her. "Take a bite of your cookie, then let's get you where you belong."

Supergirl thought about the mean things Cheetah had said, and how she'd made a mess at Capes & Cowls, and the pranks people had pulled on her. She thought about how Harley had made her look silly on "Harley's Quinntessentials." She looked like a fool! Korugar Academy was a place where she could start over.

Supergirl's laser eyes grew red as she grabbed the door handle and turned it with all her might. She struggled for a moment before she yelled, "OPEN!" Then she yanked it so hard it cracked off its hinges, leaving a clear path to the Boom Tubes.

A bright red light began flashing. "SECURITY BREACH! SECURITY BREACH!"

Cyborg and Catwoman both yawned, turned over, and went back to sleep. Granny grinned. "Ah, that hot chocolate works like a charm every time!" She leaned over to Perry and lovingly scratched behind his ears. "See, you silly little monster. That's how you do it! None of that scratching and banging! Now take care of that screeching alarm, it's giving me a headache."

Supergirl was confused as she watched Perry smash the security pad with his head. He ripped it from the wall with his sharp teeth, then proceeded to eat it, dangling wires and all. As the alarm whined off, Granny led Supergirl inside. She pulled a lever near one of the Boom Tubes, telling her, "You wait right here, dear."

Something was wrong. Terribly and awfully and for-sure wrong. But Korugar *was* a good idea, right? And Waller was just testing everyone again with the Boom Tubes threat, right? Everything was blurry and hazy, and Supergirl was having trouble thinking straight. Granny put more cookies in her hands. "Eat!" she ordered.

Supergirl stared at the cookies. But then, unable to resist, she looked through a couple of portals. She smiled when she saw families vacationing on Thanagar. The sand-surfers of Rann looked like they had no cares in the world. And the bingo players in Florida were swiping French fries from each other.

Then she peered into the portal to Apokolips. In the frightening, fiery landscape, a tall teenaged warrior batted a giant boulder with her Mega Rod. It flew over the horizon.

Supergirl was mesmerized when the warrior turned to her comrades and roared, "Female Furies—Speed Queen, Stompa, Artemiz, Mad Harriet—pair up and commence sparring!"

"Yes, Big Barda," the other teenaged warriors said in unison.

Suddenly, the Boom Tubes shook. *BOOM!* A portal, matching the one in the Super Hero High Boom Tubes room, appeared near Big Barda, who locked eyes with Supergirl and grinned.

The Furies ceased their training and Barda, a tall, strong teen sporting a dark blue-and-gold helmet, raised her weapon in victory as she announced above their cheers, "Finally! Furies, ready! For today, we conquer Earth!"

# CHAPTER 32

**S**hocked, Supergirl dropped the cookies and staggered back from the portal. Blinding lights exploded from the Boom Tubes, and high-velocity debris stung her skin. Soon after the lights died down, another explosion, this one a hundred times greater, stretched the portal to its limits, breaking down the walls. When the smoke cleared, a row of fierce Female Furies stood at attention.

"Granny! Watch out," Supergirl warned.

Granny was armed and ready for them. But wait!

Supergirl rubbed her eyes in disbelief. Before her, Granny Goodness stood tall with her shoulders back. Her kind eyes narrowed and grew ice cold as her warm voice transformed into a cackle.

"Supergirl, meet my five Female Furies!"

Granny turned toward the tall, fierce-looking warrior whose high yellow boots matched the yellow of her battle armor. "Big Barda," she said, pointing to Supergirl, "Kryptonite this one."

As Speed Queen balanced on her skates and looked on, a slow, sinister smile crossed Barda's face. Their leader pushed her way to the front and pulled out a green-glowing Kryptonite-laced Mega Rod. Supergirl was so shocked at the sight she couldn't move. Big Barda raised the rod like a baseball bat and—

*WHACK!*

The Kryptonite rod struck Supergirl against the shield on her chest. She fell to the ground. Her powers failed her. She was so weak she couldn't even use her arms. Big Barda laughed. She raised the club high over her head to finish Supergirl off—but hesitated as she glanced at Granny for approval.

"Leave her," Granny ordered. "She'll be an excellent addition to our army. So gullible and eager to please!"

Carelessly, Big Barda dropped the club next to Supergirl, just beyond her reach. Supergirl struggled to get up and push it away, but the Kryptonite was too powerful. Helpless, she crumpled back down in defeat.

Energized, Granny marshaled the Furies into formation. Like the good soldiers they were, their precision was impressive. "Furies, initiate phase two!" Granny cried in a loud, strong voice. It was clear she had done this before. "Attack!"

The Furies, led by the mighty Big Barda, marched out of the Boom Tubes room.

Granny laughed with glee. "Perry? Perry! Perry, get over here and do your job!"

Perry fetched a polished wooden chest from Artemiz the archer, whose bow and arrows were designed for deadly aim. Mad Harriet threw back her massive mess of green hair and cackled. Then, like a squire attending to his queen, the monster helped Granny strap on her armor. Before Supergirl's eyes, the transformation from a dotty old woman to the strong leader of an evil army was now complete.

"Hurry!" Granny said. "My Furies won't be able to keep the rest of them off school grounds for long. We must set the trap before those obnoxious do-gooders return."

As Perry adjusted her weapon-proof shoulder pads, Granny gazed at her reflection in one of the portals. "There's something so flattering about Apokoliptian fashion," she said coyly. "It really brings out my eyes." She glanced at Supergirl, who was still unable to respond. "Too many youngsters dismiss old people," Granny said bitterly. "People can't see past their age. But I'm a perfect example of what patience, wisdom, and a good dose of evil can accomplish!"

As if on cue, Stompa stomped to attention with her lemon-colored boots as she bowed and presented Granny with a small cube. Laced with alien technology, its lights and speakers blinked and pinged. Then she quickly backed away.

"Ah," Granny said lovingly. "My Mother Box." She cradled the box as if it were a baby. "How I've missed you!"

*PING! PING! PING!*

"Mother Box?" Supergirl recalled Barbara telling her about this tiny supercomputer with endless abilities . . . including its ability to power the Boom Tubes. "Mother Box? Barbara. Furies. Portal. Evil. Granny . . . ," Supergirl murmured.

The device and Granny's eyes both glowed yellow. Supergirl gasped in horror as her mind began to clear and the reality of the situation came into focus.

Granny? Granny Goodness? How could she have fooled all the students, the teachers, Waller . . . and her? Weakened by the Kryptonite, Supergirl didn't have the strength to fight, much less warn anyone. As she began to lose consciousness, the severity of Granny's deception became startlingly clear. The Boom Tubes had been activated. Granny's Furies were dispatched to invade Earth. The world was in danger, and there was nothing Supergirl could do about it.

Everything went dark.

# CHAPTER 33

**W**here was she?

What happened?

How much time had passed?

Supergirl lay on the ground and struggled to open her eyes. She could hear someone yelling.

Barbara?

Supergirl was confused. "Barbara? Babs, are you here? I . . . I . . . can't see you!"

"Supergirl," Barbara said, her voice coming in more clearly. "I'm talking to you via our com bracelets. I saw there was trouble at Super Hero High and I've been trying to get ahold of you. What's happening? Are you okay?"

"Oh, Babs." Supergirl mustered her strength to try to speak. "I really messed up. . . ." Her voice weakened to a whisper.

"Just stay put," Barbara ordered. "Save your energy. Don't

try to talk. I've detected your location. I'll be right there."

Supergirl attempted to laugh, but nothing came out. She wanted to tell her friend that she definitely was not going anywhere, but she passed out before she could say another word.

★

*Kara was in her room on Krypton making a birthday card for her mother. She was happy. Her mother was saying something to her.*

"You're in bad shape, but you'll survive."

"Mom?"

"No, it's me. Barbara. Your best friend. Remember?"

"Where's my mom?" Supergirl asked. Why did her head hurt so much?

Barbara knelt beside Supergirl. She couldn't hide the worry on her face. "You're safe now," Babs told her. "But you're weak. Don't push it."

Barbara picked up the Kryptonite rod that Big Barda had used on Supergirl and hurled it through the Florida Boom Tubes portal. A blue-haired retiree looked up when it landed near her bingo card. She glanced to her left, then right, before sneaking it into her purse and yelling, "BINGO!"

Barbara slung Supergirl's arm over her shoulder and led her out of the Boom Tubes room. "You once took me for a ride," she said. "Now it's my turn to return the favor. Let's go. What were you doing here?"

Supergirl struggled to regain her memory. Slowly, the horrible truth materialized. "I . . . I was trying to get to Korugar Academy," she admitted. Her cheeks flushed with shame. "Leave me and warn the others," Supergirl insisted. "I've already made a mess of everything. It's my fault Earth is being invaded. Has anyone alerted the super heroes?"

"It's not just here and it's not just you," Babs said. "The evil alien Massacre has invaded Switzerland and is intent on taking over the country. He's the worst kind of villain—he uses his speed and strength to hurt and destroy just for the fun of it. The Swiss don't have an army, so the adult Supers have come to their rescue. It's a battleground over there. That means we're on our own to fight Granny and the Furies."

"Let go of me!" Supergirl protested. "Go save yourself! I'm just a nobody, a troublemaker. I don't belong here. I never did!"

"Supergirl," Barbara said, trying to keep her temper in check. "Listen to me. You're my best friend and I need you. The world needs you. Metropolis is under siege and a huge battle is taking place. Lives are in danger. Do you understand what's happening out there?!"

Barbara stopped in front of a portal and let go of Supergirl. She took a deep breath. "If you really want to leave, then go. Look. There's Korugar Academy. Is that what you want?"

Supergirl looked at the students eating frosted cupcakes and watching movies at Korugar. They looked so happy. And why shouldn't they be? Korugar Academy wasn't being invaded by furious Furies intent on bringing them down. Then Supergirl thought about the deception of Granny Goodness, how Big Barda had knocked her out, and how the Furies seemed so angry and eager to fight to take over Earth.

"Well?" Barbara pressed. "Do you still want to go? Because if you do, I won't stop you."

Supergirl didn't answer.

# CHAPTER 34

"Babs," Supergirl said in a whisper. "Please help me to the Korugar Academy portal."

Barbara flinched as if she had been punched in the stomach. "If that's what you really want," she said without emotion.

Supergirl put her arm around Barbara and hobbled over to the portal. She stared into it for a long time, imagining herself there. Then she shut the portal and bolted it tight.

Barbara broke into a smile as she blinked back tears of relief. "That's the Supergirl I know and love," she said, hugging her best friend.

"Okay, tell me what's happening," Supergirl said, sitting down. She was still wobbly. "Tell me everything you know."

Barbara's smile disappeared. "Wonder Woman and Big Barda are in the midst of a colossal battle downtown. Look." She pulled out her B.A.T. computer and by keying in a few codes she accessed the security cameras on the street.

Supergirl's eyes widened. On-screen, Barda was thrashing her Mega Rod at Wonder Woman, who was expertly diving out of the way. In an effort to snare her in her lariat, Wonder Woman threw her Lasso of Truth at Big Barda, who somersaulted backward to evade its grip.

"This is your first offense on Earth," Wonder Woman warned. "Give yourself up right now, Barda, and your punishment won't be harsh. It's not just me you're fighting, it's all of Super Hero High—and the whole world of super heroes!"

Just then Miss Martian materialized next to Wonder Woman. She spoke so softly that Supergirl had to use her super-hearing. "What do we do?" Miss Martian was saying. "It's just us here to battle the Furies! There's some sort of situation in Switzerland and all the adult Supers are over there!"

Big Barda let go a loud long laugh. "So much for your backup!" she yelled. Just as she lunged toward Wonder Woman, the B.A.T. screen got fuzzy and then went black. Frantically, Barbara tapped it a few times. When the picture came back on, it was from another security camera, this time near Centennial Park. Supergirl was shocked to see the reptilian villain Killer Croc taking advantage of the Furies' distraction to tear apart everything in his path. There was a 5K race in progress and, in an effort to flee from the evil reptile's clutches, all the runners were breaking personal-best records.

Just as Killer Croc reached for a runner, Cheetah stepped between them. When he grabbed her instead, Katana appeared from behind a tree and threw her sword. It sliced the air and bounced off Killer Croc's hard scaly skin. This gave Cheetah enough time to retreat and distract him while Hawkgirl flew into position. With precision, Hawkgirl swooped down, catching Croc off guard. Then she pulled him up and flew off-screen. When she returned, she told Katana, "I dropped him off at the top of the tallest building in Metropolis. He can't hurt anyone up there."

Barbara's B.A.T. screen got fuzzy once more. When it cleared, Big Barda was in focus again. By now she was on the edge of another skyscraper roof and there was no place for her to go but down. "Give up!" Wonder Woman cried as she circled above her.

"Never!" Barda shouted. With a smile, she leapt off the edge of the building and in midair pulled out a pair of aero-disks to give her the power of flight.

With increasing speed, the B.A.T. computer began to broadcast scenes from all over Metropolis. Supergirl and Barbara couldn't believe the mayhem. On the ground, on rooftops—Supers and Furies were battling everywhere. Katana was employing her patented roundhouse K-kick to knock over Speed Queen. Beast Boy morphed lightning fast into several creatures big and small to confuse Stompa. Harley was getting it all on video, but was stunned when she came across a Female Fury who was doing the same thing.

"Hey! What kind of camera are you using?" Harley asked.

When Mad Harriet checked her camera, Harley pushed her into Poison Ivy, who wrapped a sturdy flex vine around her, disabling the camera and the Fury.

As it became clear that the Supers knew what they were doing, Barda called out, "Furies! Retreat!" At her signal, the army of invaders ceased their fighting and ran. Although Granny was first in command, it seemed that Big Barda was second.

Wonder Woman yelled to Poison Ivy, "It's not the citizens the Furies want. It's the Supers. Let's give them what they're asking for!"

Just then the B.A.T. screen went blank. Barbara tapped it, but nothing happened. She hit it repeatedly with the palm of her hand.

"Argggh!" she groaned. "What a time for my battery to go dead!"

"What do you think is happening?" Supergirl yelled, unsure why she was yelling. Her head was still throbbing and her body was in pain. Still, she found herself wishing she were with the rest of her peers.

"If my theory is correct," Barbara answered, "Wonder Woman is planning to lure the Furies away from Metropolis and toward Super Hero High!"

Supergirl nodded. It made sense. Wondy was trying to save the citizens of Metropolis and the world. She knew that the Supers would have the advantage if the epic battle took place at Super Hero High.

"Wait, what are you doing?" Barbara asked.

"I'm getting up," Supergirl said. "I can't fight evil sitting down, can I?"

# CHAPTER 35

Supergirl felt her strength returning, thanks in part to Barbara's constant encouragement. "Remember," Barbara said as they made their way down the deserted corridor. It was eerily quiet. "Don't rush. If you try to do too much too fast you can hurt yourself and others. Slow and steady, Supergirl. Slow and steady." She stopped and looked her best friend in the eyes. "One more piece of advice," she began. Supergirl nodded. "Double knots."

"What?"

"Your shoes. Tie your shoelaces in double knots so you won't trip and fall."

"Slow and steady. Double knots. Slow and steady," Supergirl repeated. From the window, she could see someone or something climbing up the tower toward the Amethyst. She squinted but couldn't make out what it was. Concentrating, Supergirl focused, then homed in on the figure. Slowly, things started coming into focus.

"Barbara!" she yelled. "It's Granny Goodness!"

"Well, I see your vocal cords are at full strength," Barbara said, rubbing her ear. "I'll alert the other Supers. Don't go anywhere. You're not one hundred percent back yet!"

Supergirl watched Babs run down the hallway. She wanted to be out there, stopping Granny, but instead she had to wait for her full powers to return—if they ever would. Funny, Supergirl used to wish she'd never had super powers. Now she would have given anything to have them back.

She was heartened to find her super-vision getting stronger. Perry and Granny were now visible and she could see that Perry was clutching an Apokoliptian tech device— the Mother Box!

Supergirl shut her eyes and struggled to hear what they were saying. At first everything was jumbled. She tried to clear her head. "Slow and steady," she could hear Barbara reminding her. Then she heard another voice. . . .

"Hurry, you little monster!" Granny growled as she continued her climb. "Perry, don't you dare drop that. It's our key to controlling those pesky teen super heroes, and claiming Super Hero High as ours!"

Supergirl's eyes fluttered open just in time to see the two place the device on the top of the tower. Instantly, the Amethyst began to glow with a strange, sickly yellow light. Supergirl couldn't take her eyes off it.

The glow slowly began to spread outward as Granny raised her arms in triumph. Supergirl could hear her chant, "Force of Apokolips! Power of Gemworld's Amethyst! Be mine, all mine!"

With a lightning bolt flash, the glow from the Amethyst radiated to Granny Goodness, causing her whole body to emanate a bright yellow light. Supergirl cringed as Granny cackled with delight.

There was a rustling sound and then over the school's PA system, a voice blasted. "Is this on? Can you hear me? Can you hear me now?" Supergirl could hear Granny laughing, then cooing gleefully, "Congratulations, students! You're currently coming under the control of a good ole Granny brainwashing!"

★

"Supergirl!" Barbara was out of breath as she rushed toward her. "It's horrible out there. The Furies and Big Barda are battling the Supers. They've had multiple injuries . . . but so have we. Super Hero High's emergency room is overflowing. And now Granny has taken over the Amethyst and is transmitting a mind-control device over the school.

"The timing is terrible—Wonder Woman and the Supers are headed back here, trying to lure the Furies away from Metropolis!"

Supergirl was stunned. It was worse than she had thought possible.

"My mini-computer," Barbara groaned. "It's dead, and

I can't monitor how close the Supers are to arriving."

"The library!" Supergirl cried. "There are computers in the library."

With each step they took, Supergirl felt herself getting stronger. By the time they reached the library she was able to walk normally. Barbara ran up to the checkout desk's computer. Bypassing the password, she began to type furiously. Within seconds Barbara had accessed the secret numbers embedded in the Dewey decimal classification system that only librarians were privy to. Using those, she was able to hack into the Super Hero High security cameras.

Supergirl shook her head in disbelief. By now most of the Supers were back at the school. What she saw was a nightmare as the screen filled with scenes from around campus. Everywhere, students were succumbing to Granny's trance as the old lady broadcast over the loudspeaker, "My darlings, as part of my army, you'll pave the way for our supreme ruler, Darkseid of Apokolips, to conquer Earth!"

There were several clicking noises as the computer screen showed other security-camera areas. Supergirl gasped when she saw a beam of light wash over Harley. "Don't look at it," she called out even though she knew her friend couldn't hear her. "Don't look at it, Harley! Don't look!"

Harley looked up at the light and was instantly brought under a trance, her eyes glowing yellow. Supergirl witnessed Bumblebee staggering backward to avoid the light, but she couldn't get far enough away fast enough. In scene after scene, the yellow light rolled over Super Hero High like a tidal wave. No one was immune.

"We'll be safe in the IT Annex," Barbara said as they ran from the library, where the yellow light was beginning to seep in. "I've made sure that its walls are quadruple quintillion reinforced. If I can get there, I may be able to help shut down Granny's mind-control light."

Supergirl's head and heart were ready for battle, but her body wasn't. She began to think about her planet exploding and the loss of her parents. She thought about the Kents taking her in, and about the betrayal by Granny Goodness, and let out a small sob.

As if reading her mind, Barbara said, "She fooled us all, Supergirl, not just you. Don't blame yourself."

Supergirl let this sink in. It was true. Granny had tricked everyone, beginning with Principal Waller, who had hired her. But now that the real Granny was revealed, something had to be done.

The more Supergirl thought about it, the angrier she got. Feeling her strength returning in full force, she put her hands on her hips and announced, "We have to stop Granny Goodness and save the world!"

Barbara nodded, laughing. "Well, yeah," she said. "That's the goal."

★

Once in the IT Annex, Barbara set to work.

"How can I help?" Supergirl asked.

"I've got this," Babs said. "I've calculated the frequency of Granny's device and created a de-trancer. There's only one problem."

On Barbara's massive bank of computer screens, Supergirl could see more and more of her friends falling under Granny's control. The Furies were gleefully rounding them up.

"I need a solidified igneous rock formed by molten magma to counteract the power and range of the Amethyst," Barbara said.

"You need a what?" Supergirl asked.

"I need a crystal," said Barbara. "One that can conduct energy. But where can I find one now?"

Without hesitation, Supergirl removed the crystal from her necklace.

"Would this work?" she asked, handing it to Barbara.

Her friend looked at her, surprised. "This is from your mother?"

Supergirl nodded. "Take it," she insisted, putting the crystal in Barbara's hand. Supergirl stood tall and said, "The world needs it more than I do."

Barbara smiled as she inserted Supergirl's crystal into the device.

"POW! De-trancing on!" Babs declared. Then she clipped a small pair of earrings to Supergirl's ears. "These will keep you safe from Granny's trance. To release a Super from the trance, just point this at them and push the button." She handed the device to Supergirl, adding, "You can fly and get to places and people I can't. I'm counting on you, Supergirl. We all are."

# CHAPTER 36

"What was that?" Supergirl asked, jumping up.

"I don't hear anything," Barbara said. She took off her glasses and rubbed her eyes. It had been a long day and there was no end in sight.

Supergirl tilted her head to listen. "It's Granny. They're heading this way!"

"We can bolt the IT Annex doors from the inside," Barbara said, quickly reprogramming the security code.

"Barda's strong. So are the rest of the Furies," Supergirl noted. "They're going to get in here to bypass all the security systems you've put in place."

Barbara shook her head. "All this tech equipment is useless if you don't know what to do with it—and because I created most of it myself, I'm the only one who knows how it works. C'mon, we can get out this way."

Crawling through the school's massive air vents,

Supergirl and Barbara were able to spy on Granny marching triumphantly down the hall, Perry trotting by her side. The Furies all followed in formation behind her—all but one, who slipped out of line.

Big Barda paused to stare at a display case featuring paintings and art created by the students. She raised her Mega Rod in the air, about to smash it to pieces, but then stopped herself. Gently setting it down, she examined a cherry blossom tree that Katana had painted, the Tamaran flowers lovingly shaded by Starfire, and Star Sapphire's Cupid surrounded by glittery diamond hearts.

Granny snapped her fingers in front of Barda's face. "Apokolips to Barda. Are those paint splatters more interesting than me?"

Barda blubbered, "No, it's just—the Supers who go to school here, in their studies, they get to make beautiful things like this?"

Granny laughed like she'd just heard the funniest joke in the universe. "Silly girl. Who needs art when you can have power? Let's go! We have work to do if we're going to rule the world."

With a last longing look at the showcase, Barda let out a sigh, then rushed to catch up with the others.

★

With Granny and her five fierce Furies storming the school, Barbara was able to track their whereabouts on her computer watch, and Supergirl was able to listen in on them. As they trailed behind them, Supergirl de-tranced several Supers. Still, there were many more she needed to get to.

"De-trancing one at a time will take too long," Barbara whispered in a panic. "Your crystal is working great, but I wish we had something even more powerful."

"Wait!" Supergirl exclaimed. "What about the Amethyst?"

Barbara thought about it, then nodded. "Yes! If Granny can use the Amethyst to amplify her powers, I can use it too. I'll just need to plug the de-trancer into it! But I need to get there without Granny and her Furies trying to stop me."

Supergirl raised her hand. "I can create a distraction," she said, bending down to double-knot her shoelaces and adding a third knot for good measure.

"You might not be ready yet," Barbara warned. "We don't know if you have your full powers. . . ."

Before she could finish her sentence, Supergirl was gone.

With laser focus, Supergirl zipped toward the Furies, angering Granny and startling Big Barda. They were now outside in the courtyard, where they were amassing the Supers, lined up in tidy rows with blank looks on their faces. Never had Supergirl seen Beast Boy so still, or Harley not talking—and there were teachers, too. Crazy Quilt,

Liberty Belle, and Mr. Fox were among them.

Supergirl flew around the scene, swooping lower with each pass. "Are you looking for something to do?" she called out, taunting Granny and her army. "Because I'm bored."

Granny's steely eyes narrowed. "Power of Apokolips!" she shouted, raising her arms high in the air. "Control this annoying gnat of a girl!"

The yellow light washed over Supergirl. She gasped. Her body jerked, and suddenly she dropped to the ground, her face blank like the others'.

Granny Goodness's laugh echoed between the buildings. "Oh, that was just too easy," she said, scratching Perry behind the ears. "Come on, Furies, let's finish this school off. We'll merge the Super Hero High teens with our Furies and then attack Metropolis from all sides. Then it's on to every major city in the world, ending in Switzerland to take care of that clod Massacre. What a dupe! By then our army will be so big we can rule the world!"

Barda smiled and nodded. Perry drooled, and the Furies lifted their heads in triumph as they surveyed the Supers standing before them at attention.

"Not so fast, Granny!"

Granny whipped around. "You?!" she cried.

"Yes, me," Supergirl said calmly. She was holding a car above her head.

A swath of yellow light hit Supergirl, but she didn't flinch. Her de-trancing earrings were doing their job. "I was never under your power," Supergirl explained. "But I needed to know your plans." With that, she tossed the car at Granny, but Big Barda stepped in and batted it away.

"GET HER!" Granny cried.

Big Barda led the charge, with her compatriots following close behind. Soon the Furies were all in pursuit of Supergirl. As she led them away from the Amethyst Tower, Barbara began her ascent toward the gem.

Though they were fast and cunning and strong, the Furies were no match for Supergirl. Any self-doubt she once had was now gone, and it showed. For the first time in her life, Supergirl felt in full control of her powers. Without hesitation, she flew with lightning speed around the Furies, causing massive confusion among the ranks as their weapons shot at one another and they yelled in anger and frustration.

At the same time, Supergirl kept a watchful eye on her best friend, who was nearing the top of the tower. Barbara replaced her grappling hook with the B.A.T. grappling gun calibrated for distance and strength. With expert precision, she aimed and fired it upward toward the massive prongs that secured the Amethyst. The hook caught the metal with a loud clang that rang across the school. Alerted, Artemiz, who was about to shoot Supergirl with her bow and arrow, stopped and grinned. Then she turned and instead aimed at Barbara Gordon.

Before Supergirl could respond, she saw Gorilla Grodd

exit a terrace door, grab a rope from one of the school flags, and swing across the building, letting out a fierce gorilla yell.

Her jaw dropped when Grodd positioned himself between Artemiz's arrow and Barbara.

"Noooooo!" Barbara shouted, horrified, when the arrow meant for her struck the former vice principal. He plummeted, landing with a thud that shook the ground.

Artemiz readied another arrow and took aim at Barbara. Supergirl raised her com bracelet. "Barbara," she yelled. "Watch out! Another arrow is headed your way!"

Furies descended upon Supergirl as she looked over at the tower in time to see Barbara thrust herself over the side of the building onto the roof. With gymnastic skills worthy of Harley Quinn, Barbara flipped up to the Amethyst and in a single motion plugged her de-trancer into it.

A loud *BOOM!* could be heard throughout the city as the de-trancer began to emit a blue light that overtook Granny's yellow light, bathing Super Hero High in hope.

All was good! Or was it?

Bumblebee was at Grodd's side, trying to revive him. "I'm sorry I didn't trust you!" she cried when he didn't move. The Flash and Hawkgirl looked stricken, too, but their battle was not over yet.

# CHAPTER 37

As the soothing blue light blanketed the Supers, they came out of their trances. Some were angry, some were confused, some were tired. All were ready to fight back.

Granny's face contorted at the sight of her evil plan unraveling. She raised her fists in the air and yelled, "FURIES! ATTACK!"

The Furies turned away from Supergirl and before she could stop them, they spread out, each taking on a Super or two. They were well trained. Supergirl knew this, having observed them via the Boom Tubes portals. Yet her fellow Super Hero High students had studied under Wildcat and Mr. Fox, and the other distinguished teachers, all heroes themselves. And they were led by none other than Amanda "The Wall" Waller, who was a force to be reckoned with in any universe.

Supergirl watched with amazement as Miss Martian—

normally so shy that it made others uncomfortable—called out in a voice loud and clear, "Don't mess with Super Hero High, you horrible Furies!" as she charged into battle.

Speed Queen, who had been running head-on toward The Flash, suddenly fell sprawling to the ground when the invisible Miss Martian inserted herself between the two, tripping her.

Humiliated, an angry Speed Queen got up and fled. "Good riddance!" Miss Martian called after her. Giddy, she hugged The Flash, but after a second he was hugging himself with Miss Martian nowhere to be seen.

Beast Boy had turned into a snake to get close to Stompa. Just as she was about to crush him, he became a fire-breathing dragon.

"Excuse me, but who were you planning to stomp?" he roared, fire blazing from his mouth as Stompa backed away.

Meanwhile, Artemiz and Katana were slowly circling each other at a distance, getting closer with each step. Artemiz had her bow and arrows at the ready and trained on Katana. Katana had one hand out toward her opponent, beckoning her, and held her sword aloft with the other.

"Give me what you've got," Katana taunted. "I'm not afraid of you."

Artemiz's eyes narrowed. "Well, you should be," she said, releasing several arrows at once.

"Katana, watch out!" Beast Boy yelled as he battled Stompa.

"I got this!" Katana assured him.

She spun, ducking some arrows while slashing others to bits with her sword, then finally grabbing one with her free hand.

"I think this belongs to you?" Katana said, pinning Artemiz to the ground with an arrow through her tunic.

In another corner of the campus, Supergirl could see Harley doing whip-fast backflips and then hitting a surprised Mad Harriet with her mega mallet in one hand while taking a video with her other. But with each hit, Mad Harriet merely laughed and bounced back up. Then she lunged toward Harley.

Before she made contact, Cheetah leapt in and growled, "Harley, you're gonna want to get this on video!"

"You got it!" Harley called out as Mad Harriet released razor-sharp claws and went after Cheetah. But Cheetah was too fast. "Is that the best you've got?" she sneered as she climbed up a trellis wall.

In a blind rage, Mad Harriet screamed and chased her up the trellis, unaware that Poison Ivy was nearby. The girl with the green thumb had mutated the vines to grow spikes and capture the next person who touched them.

"Get off me!" Mad Harriet growled as the vines twisted tight around her, pinning her down. "Leave me alone!"

"Yes!" Cheetah and Poison Ivy yelled as they high-fived.

"You get that?" Cheetah asked Harley as Mad Harriet stewed, all wrapped up with nowhere to go.

"Got it!" Harley yelled back.

Supergirl looked up to see Bumblebee flying circles above them, letting out her most powerful bee sting ever. It was so powerful that she flew backward, knocking over Speed Queen, who had rejoined the fight and had Frost cornered. From behind a row of trash cans, Parasite appeared carrying a bucket and armed with brooms and mops he had turned into offensive weapons. But try as he might to land a blow, Speed Queen was too quick for him.

"Ready?" Parasite called out to Frost.

"Ready!" Frost replied as the janitor emptied a bucket of dirty mop water at Speed Queen's feet.

"I'm not afraid of a little water," Speed Queen laughed, narrowing her eyes and getting into position to race toward Frost.

"You may not be afraid of water, but what about a little ice?" Frost asked, freezing the water and causing Speed Queen to slip and fall. She fell again and again, unable to get up from the slick ice.

As Green Lantern and Star Sapphire moved in to help secure Speed Queen, Harley got it all on video.

Hovering behind the Statue of Justice, Supergirl watched the fight unfold. She reached for her necklace, but it wasn't there. Panic overcame her until she remembered that she had given it to Barbara to fuel the de-trancer. As proud as she was about how well the Supers were doing, Supergirl knew that it was because of her that there was a battle in the first place. If she hadn't tried to access the forbidden Boom Tubes, none of this would have happened.

It looked like the Supers were doing just fine without her. "Supergirl?"

A familiar friendly voice called out to her. Supergirl looked up to see Granny Goodness standing atop the Tower. She was no longer wearing her battle armor and her evil face had softened. She smoothed out a crease in her old-fashioned skirt. Granny was holding her cookie jar.

"Supergirl, so glad you're safe," she said. "You look like you could use a cookie. Dear, why don't you come with me and make something of yourself. Join the family. . . ."

"Family?" Supergirl said, thinking of her mother and father. Suddenly, she was no longer Supergirl, super hero. She was Kara from Krypton, wondering what she was doing in the middle of an epic battle and wishing she were anywhere else.

# CHAPTER 38

As the battle raged around them, Granny Goodness and Supergirl almost didn't notice that they could no longer hear the cries of victory or the pain of defeat. Instead, it was as if the world had stopped and it was just the two of them: a fierce old woman and a fearful teen.

"We're the same, us orphans," Granny reminded her. "Join me, Supergirl, and you too can be in Darkseid's army. You can command the Furies with me! Your parents never wanted you to be alone and lonely."

It was true—Supergirl's parents *hadn't* wanted her to be alone or lonely. That was why they'd sent her to Earth. In that moment, all Supergirl had been through flashed before her. What she had lost . . . and what she'd gained. Perhaps she couldn't trust Granny Goodness, but there were others who she believed in, and who believed in her.

Suddenly, Supergirl knew what she must do. Her mother's voice echoed in her mind: "Always do your best, Kara, and you'll be fine. I promise. You have the heart of a hero. "

She heard Barbara saying, "Gut-check it. What does your heart say?"

Any doubt Kara Zor-El had harbored disappeared. Supergirl nodded at Granny. "You're right," she said. "I don't want to be alone."

Granny smiled and offered her a cookie.

"But I don't want to be with you, or the Furies, or Darkseid," Supergirl said confidently with a smile.

In an instant, Granny's own sweet smile turned sinister. She whipped around and was suddenly dressed as Darkseid's loyal warrior once more. Catching Supergirl off guard, Granny put her into a headlock. "How dare you speak of Darkseid like that?" she demanded. "You're too weak to be one of my Furies anyway. I may as well just get rid of you right now!"

Supergirl gasped. "Oooh, look at Perry, so cute!" she wheezed.

When Granny turned, Supergirl twisted out of her grasp. The two stood facing each other, their jaws tight and their fists clenched, both in a fighting stance.

"Let's not argue," Granny said, slipping into her sweet voice once more. "I wasn't really going to hurt you. I'm just doing my job."

"Really?" Supergirl said sarcastically.

"Yes, really," Granny said. "Before Waller had the Boom Tubes sealed off, I could come and go as I pleased, recruiting young Supers to be in Darkseid's army. I was especially fond of lonely, naive orphans who were trying to find their place in the world. Poor dears lost their family and friends. But then, you know what that's like, don't you, Kara Zor-El of the doomed planet Krypton?

"There are rule followers, rule breakers, and rule makers," Granny was saying. Supergirl nodded as she backed up. Then she took a deep breath and was about to speed recklessly ahead when the old woman, who was more powerful and quicker than her Furies, blasted a yellow mind-control beam at her. Supergirl countered with her heat vision, which coupled with Barbara's de-trancer earrings, blocked the ghastly light. Still, something was wrong. Supergirl recalled Barbara's advice to go slow and steady.

Taking heed, Supergirl slowed and focused, whipping around and tackling Granny. "I can see through walls and now I can see through you!" she yelled as the two fought.

"Barda!" Granny ordered. "Come here! Now!"

Big Barda was fast. She lunged toward Supergirl, who released Granny, knowing she couldn't hold on to her *and* fight the Fury.

"Catch me if you can," Supergirl said as she flew toward the obstacle course. Hovering on her aero-disks, Barda was in fast pursuit. Supergirl soared toward the poles. At the last second, she dived out of the way and her nemesis slammed into the steel column—but this didn't stop her. Supergirl deftly flew up and down around the lasers with a skill and precision she'd never employed before. Barda tried to follow, but a laser zapped her leg, causing her to grab it and feel actual pain.

Still, the chase did not cease. In the tunnel, Supergirl dodged the cannons as Barda was struck hard by a stream of the sticky, gooey green goop. As Barda attempted to shake it off, Supergirl soared to the finish line, hitting the button with her fist as she passed. The electronic score tallied 100!

Supergirl wished Barbara were here to see it. Just then she heard a voice.

"Supergirl!"

"Babs?" Supergirl said into her com bracelet. "You should have seen what just happened."

"I did!" Barbara said, tapping her on the shoulder.

Supergirl looked at her bracelet, then at Barbara standing next to her. Confusion gave way to a smile.

"I was listening in on our com bracelet," Barbara explained. "So I knew where you were and what was happening. After I set up a security force field around the school to keep the Furies from escaping, I headed straight here."

There was a noise coming from the tunnel. Both girls looked over in time to see a battered, goop-covered Barda stagger toward them, then collapse.

Wonder Woman flew in, looked at the score, and said, "Way to go, Supergirl! But do you mind? Granny is still on the loose, and I could use some help saving the world."

Supergirl was the first to spot Granny and Perry racing across the Tower's terrace toward the Amethyst. Cradled under Granny's arm was something familiar—a cookie jar.

"Where are you going with those cookies?" Supergirl called out as she and Wonder Woman flew toward her.

Granny stopped but didn't turn around, allowing Perry to charge recklessly toward them. In a heartbeat Wonder Woman whipped out her lasso, catching him in the loop. As she cinched the rope, Perry exploded into a dozen small, harmless green parademons. Like roaches, the Perrys ran here and there, bumping into everything, including one another.

With the mini Perrys causing a distraction, Granny headed for the Amethyst. Supergirl flew toward her, but with a powerful stroke of her arm, Granny sent her sprawling across the terrace, crashing several stories down to the ground. Stunned, Supergirl staggered to her feet. Granny grinned and held her cookie jar aloft.

"This jar is, in reality, a Granny grenade!" she said, her cackle echoing around Super Hero High. "Did you really think I liked baking that much?"

As she continued laughing at her own joke, Supergirl could see Barbara sneaking up behind Granny Goodness. . . .

# CHAPTER 39

**W**ith the stealth of Cheetah, the agility of Katana, and the confidence of Wonder Woman, Barbara silently crept up behind Granny and got into position. She unfurled a B.A.T. computer cable and lassoed the old lady's ankles, bringing her crashing down. Granny roared, and in a fit of anger twisted the cable with her bare hands until it snapped.

This gave Supergirl enough time to pull a flagpole out of the ground and fly to the terrace. As Barbara distracted Granny, Supergirl bent the steel pole and wrapped it securely around the old lady. Granny struggled against the metal binding, dropping her cookie jar. Slowly, it rolled over to the very edge of the terrace and teetered back and forth, threatening to fall.

Supergirl held her breath.

Barbara gasped.

Granny's face lit up.

"When that hits the ground, kaboom!" Granny Goodness boasted. "My cookie jar has the capacity to destroy the entire city of Metropolis, and even a few of the suburbs!"

Then, Granny puffed out her cheeks and blew the cookie jar off the ledge.

Supergirl raced to stop the cookie-jar bomb before it hit the ground. Just as she was about to grab it, someone else got there first.

"Wonder Woman!" Supergirl shouted.

"That's me!" Wonder Woman confirmed. Both friends smiled. But seconds later, their smiles disappeared. The jar began to beep. Slowly at first, then faster and faster.

"It's going to explode!" Babs cried.

Without hesitation, Supergirl grabbed the cookie jar from Wondy. She tucked it under her arm and soared straight up, ignoring Barbara and Wonder Woman yelling, "No, Supergirl, nooooooo!"

Never in her life had Supergirl been so scared, or so sure of what she had to do. As she pierced the clouds, the beeping grew louder and faster, and planet Earth got smaller. Supergirl pushed herself past her limits, rocketing out of Earth's atmosphere, and then, when the lights on the bomb turned red, she tossed the cookie jar with all her might into the emptiness of space.

The explosion was huge. For the first time since her escape from Krypton, Supergirl was at peace. Though her hair was practically standing upright, her heart was beating fast and strong. At last, Supergirl knew what it meant to be a super hero.

★

Turning around, Supergirl took her time heading back to Earth, passing through the rain of cookies and stardust that littered the sky. She could hear crying as she neared Super Hero High. What had happened? she wondered. Had they lost the battle?

As she got closer, cries turned to cheers when Hawkgirl pointed up and yelled, "It's her! Supergirl lives!"

"Supergirl saved the day!" Cyborg called out.

"Smile, Supergirl!" Harley yelled, training her camera on her.

Everyone was ecstatic. Even Cheetah was heard saying, "I always knew she had it in her."

As she was carried on the shoulders of her fellow Supers, she saw Bumblebee with Mr. Grodd. "I have to keep saying it. I am sooooooo sorry," Bumblebee was saying. "I should never have accused you of being anything but a good gorilla."

Barbara cut in to say, "Vice Principal Grodd, you saved my life!"

Embarrassed, the gorilla tried to shake off their apologies and compliments, but he reluctantly relented and awkwardly let them hug him.

★

Principal Waller, Wonder Woman, Barbara Gordon, and Supergirl gathered in the Boom Tubes room. Granny and four of her Furies were secured in handcuffs as Beast Boy, who had turned into a fierce dog, guarded them and the many tiny Perrys, who were tumbling around and playing in hamster cages. With a hard yank on the lever, Waller sent them all to the Belle Reve Penitentiary and Juvenile Detention Center.

"You can never stop Darkseid!" Granny's voice echoed through the Boom Tubes portal until there was silence.

"Wait a minute! Where's Big Barda?" Waller asked.

"I'll find her," Supergirl volunteered.

Using her X-ray vision, she scanned the school and was surprised by what she saw.

"Barda!" Supergirl hollered, walking slowly toward her, ready for anything.

Big Barda was gently picking up a sculpture that had fallen to the ground during the battle. She placed it securely back on its pedestal.

"That's all well and good, Barda," Supergirl said softly. "But it's time to go."

Big Barda did not put up a fight. In silence the two walked side by side back to the Boom Tubes. When they got there, Grodd picked up a Super Hero High brochure and slipped it to Barda. "Some reading material for your ride to Belle Reve," he said with a wink.

Barda looked down at the brochure and shook her head.

"Something tells me you could have done a lot more damage than you did," Supergirl told her. "Maybe, after paying for your crimes, you'll see a way to use your power for good . . . to help your friends."

Barda scowled and said bitterly, "I don't have friends."

Supergirl smiled warmly. "It may seem that way, for now," she said. "I was alone when I arrived here, as well. You might come around to seeing what Earth has to offer, like I did."

"Unlikely," Barda said sullenly. "This place is terrible."

Supergirl noticed that Big Barda was holding tight to the brochure.

★

After Principal Waller sent Big Barda through the same Boom Tubes portal Granny Goodness and her Furies used to get to the Belle Reve detention center, the heroes of Super Hero High began to scatter. Before she left, Barbara pressed something into the palm of Supergirl's hand. Supergirl looked down to see the familiar warm glow of her crystal and reattached it to her necklace, where it belonged.

"Are you here to help me seal the Boom Tubes door once and for all?" Principal Waller asked. They were the only two left.

Supergirl nodded. "But first, there's something I'd like to ask you."

"What is it?" said Waller.

Supergirl looked serious. "May I see the Krypton portal?"

The Wall stood silent and then said in an uncharacteristically kind voice, "Supergirl, you know there's nothing there. The planet was completely destroyed."

Supergirl nodded. "I know. But I need to see it for myself."

Waller nodded and stepped aside. Supergirl took a deep breath and slowly walked toward the Krypton portal and lifted the black cloth that covered it. After staring for a long while, she finally said, "You were right, there's nothing left." The pain in her heart was searing. "Everything is gone." Her voice was trembling. "Everything was destroyed when my planet exploded."

"Not everything," Waller said. "There's something that wasn't destroyed. Something very valuable that meant a lot to your parents."

Supergirl's eyes were moist. Though she could lift mountains, outrun trains, and fly faster than a comet, she couldn't stop her tears from flowing. "What is it?" she asked. "What could possibly be left?"

"You," Waller said. "Supergirl, as long as you are here, so is Krypton. It lives on in your mind, in your heart, and in your deeds."

Though the portal was dark, Supergirl could hear her mother saying, "Always do your best, Kara, and you'll be fine. I promise."

Waller walked Supergirl to another portal. They could see

Korugar Academy in session. "Well?" she asked.

Supergirl took a deep breath and faced Waller. "I've seen enough. Now it's time for me to get back to school. This school. Super Hero High is where I belong. I have a lot to learn, and there's no better time to start than right now."

# EPILOGUE

At the assembly, Waller praised the students, teachers, and staff, many of whom were bandaged up or wearing their casts with pride. When Supergirl nodded to newly promoted Executive Janitor Parasite, he just kept sweeping, putting his head down to hide his smile.

"Special thanks goes to Wonder Woman, who led the fight against the Furies, and to Bumblebee, Hawkgirl, and The Flash, who were on the case from the start," Principal Waller continued. "A special commendation goes to Vice Principal Grodd, who acted nobly and is a role model for us all."

Commissioner Gordon led the applause as Grodd stood awkwardly. Bumblebee flew onstage and handed him a basket filled with fresh bamboo.

From her seat, Supergirl looked up to the rafters, where Barbara was perched, wearing the black outfit Katana had made for her.

"And now," Waller was saying, "I'd like to introduce our Super Hero of the Month. Someone who, in a short time, has proven that it's not enough just to have superpowers, it's what you do with them that matters. Someone who risked her life to save others, and who tries her best at everything she does . . . Supergirl, join me onstage!"

The room broke into thunderous applause. Stunned, Supergirl thought her heart was so full it might explode. As Waller continued her speech, Supergirl whispered into her com bracelet, "Babs, you helped me become who I am. You helped save the world from Granny Goodness and her army. You deserve to be up here, too."

"In my dreams, Supergirl," Barbara replied wistfully. "In my dreams."

"Supergirl," The Wall said, pushing her toward the microphone. "Would you like to say a few words?"

Supergirl nodded. The room hushed as she held on to her crystal necklace. It began to glow brighter than it ever had before.

"It was all of us in this room who helped bring down Granny Goodness and the Furies," Supergirl began as she looked at her friends. Bumblebee leaned forward. Katana sat tall. Hawkgirl smiled. Poison Ivy nodded. Wonder Woman waved. Harley videotaped. "But there is one person who always goes unrecognized, yet was instrumental in the battle against evil. Someone who has the heart of a super hero."

Supergirl put her hand over the microphone and whispered something to Principal Waller, who listened seriously, nodded, and then took a step back.

Supergirl lit up and said loudly and proudly, "With the approval of the faculty and school administration, I would like to welcome our newest student to Super Hero High! Batgirl!"

When the figure dressed in black swung down from the rafters and landed onstage, there was silence and confusion.

"Who's that?" Cyborg asked.

Katana couldn't keep the secret any longer. She leapt up and yelled, "Hey, everyone, it's Barbara Gordon!"

The Supers and all the teachers murmured, then cheered— all except for one person who sat stunned, staring at the girl in the Batgirl costume.

"Oh, uh. Hi, Dad," Batgirl said, waving nervously to Commissioner Gordon. "Um, I can explain. . . ."

Mieke Kramer

Lisa Yee's debut novel, *Millicent Min, Girl Genius*, won the prestigious Sid Fleischman Humor Award. With nearly two million books in print, her other novels for young readers include *Stanford Wong Flunks Big-Time*; *Absolutely Maybe*; *Bobby vs. Girls (Accidentally)*; *Bobby the Brave (Sometimes)*; *Warp Speed*; *The Kidney Hypothetical, Or How to Ruin Your Life in Seven Days*; and American Girl's Kanani books, *Good Luck, Ivy*, and the 2016 Girl of the Year books. Lisa has been a Thurber House Children's Writer-in-Residence, and her books have been named an NPR Best Summer Read, a *Sports Illustrated Kids* Hot Summer Read, and a *USA Today* Critics' Pick, among other accolades. Visit Lisa at LisaYee.com.

# Super Powers!
# Super Problems!

## AN ORIGINAL GRAPHIC NOVEL
Meet the students of Super Hero High in this new action-packed adventure.

**WRITTEN BY SHEA FONTANA    ART BY YANCEY LABAT**

dcsuperherogirls.co